MS

"Linda,
what is wrong with you?"

"What's wrong with me is you! Being so nice, looking so ... so ... " She gestured, at a loss for words. "Making me want you so, when I can't have you," she added helplessly, admitting finally what she had sworn never to let him know.

Jeff rushed toward her. "Darling, here I am, you can have me. You always could."

"No," she said desperately.

"Yes, damn it, yes," he insisted, pushing her against the wall, crushing her between it and his body. "Feel me, darling. Can't you let go, Linda, and give us what we both need?"

Dear Reader:

As the months go by, we continue to receive word from you that SECOND CHANCE AT LOVE romances are providing you with the kind of romantic entertainment you're looking for. In your letters you've voiced enthusiastic support for SECOND CHANCE AT LOVE, you've shared your thoughts on how personally meaningful the books are, and you've suggested ideas and changes for future books. Although we can't always reply to your letters as quickly as we'd like, please be assured that we appreciate your comments. Your thoughts are all-important to us!

We're glad many of you have come to associate SECOND CHANCE AT LOVE books with our butterfly trademark. We think the butterfly is a perfect symbol of the reaffirmation of life and thrilling new love that SECOND CHANCE AT LOVE heroines and heroes find together in each story. We hope you keep asking for the ''butterfly books,'' and that, when you buy one—whether by a favorite author or a talented new writer—you're sure of a good read. You can trust all SECOND CHANCE AT LOVE books to live up to the high standards of romantic fiction you've come to expect.

So happy reading, and keep your letters coming!

With warm wishes,

Ellen Edwards

Ellen Edwards
SECOND CHANCE AT LOVE
The Berkley/Jove Publishing Group
200 Madison Avenue
New York, NY 10016

P. S. Everyone at SECOND CHANCE AT LOVE wishes you a *very* romantic Valentine's Day.

TRIAL BY FIRE
FAYE MORGAN

**SECOND CHANCE AT LOVE
BOOK**

For my husband, Ken,
cheerleader, critic, friend.

Chapter One

LINDA REDFIELD GATHERED the pile of manila folders from the table and thrust them into her briefcase in disgust. She had just lost her fourth case in a row to the same opponent. She snapped the clasp shut and looked out the leaded window of the courtroom, idly wondering what to do about lunch, while still preoccupied with her most recent defeat.

Linda had been a legal-aid attorney for two years, since graduating from law school. Her clients were the poor, the disenfranchised, the hopeless. To overcome those disadvantages was enough of an uphill battle without being pitted against the corporate might of Blackfoot Enterprises and its representative—Jefferson T. Langford.

Linda watched covertly as he smoothed his thick red-gold hair and adjusted his tie. He made a comment to his clerk, and the boy laughed. Slipping an expensive-looking pen into his lapel pocket, Langford flipped through a black leather notebook as he and the boy walked down the center aisle, and Linda followed the progress of the tall slim form until both men had disappeared through the double doors into the hall.

"Studying the crown prince?" Maggie's voice said behind her, and Linda jumped.

"The face of mine enemy," Linda responded dryly, turning to look at her colleague, who regarded her with an arch smile.

"Don't tell me how it came out. Let me guess," Maggie said, wide-eyed.

Linda picked up her bags. "Very funny. You saw the briefs. You know I had no case. Just once I'd like to go up against that guy with something substantial."

Maggie walked with her toward the elevators. "I don't think it would make any difference. How could you combat that elegance and grace, those Boston-inflected *A*'s, screaming nannies, prep school, and Harvard Law? 'To the manner born,' I believe the expression is. And *whatever* the manner is, he's got it, and the juries love it." She detached an envelope from her clipboard. "I have to file this in Superior Court before noon. Meet me downstairs and we'll go to lunch—someplace fancy, to cheer you up a little."

Linda nodded and smiled, rounding the corner to get to the elevator. Most of the courtroom crowd had already gone down, and she was alone as she pressed the button. Just as the doors were closing Jefferson Langford walked up and stepped between them.

"Mr. Langford," Linda said, unnerved to have the subject of her recent conversation appear so suddenly.

"You did a fine job with an impossible task today, Ms. Redfield," he said kindly. "You're to be complimented."

If anyone else had said it, Linda would have accepted

the praise graciously. But she didn't want to be patronized, and replied, "But I lost anyway...as usual."

He shrugged slightly. "We can't be winners all the time."

"Except you, Mr. Langford," she said pointedly. "You can be a winner all the time."

A small frown appeared between his amber brows, as if he were puzzled. "I've lost cases."

Linda shook her head as they reached the ground floor. "Not to me."

They lingered in the dim, cool lobby. "You haven't had any material to work with," Langford said. "You used the only possible argument, constructive eviction, and you know as well as I do that Blackfoot maintains those apartments in good condition. You need a client who pays his rent and doesn't disappear, debt-ridden, in the middle of the night." He shifted his weight, leaning against the marble column at the foot of the wide central staircase. "In addition, Judge Casey has heard too many landlord-tenant cases with legal-aid attorneys waving the statute book under his nose and crying constructive eviction. He doesn't exactly rank that argument with Darrow's defense at the Monkey Trial." He spread his hands eloquently. "You could beat me in a fair fight."

Though she knew he was right, his very reasonableness made her more obstinate. "No, I couldn't. I haven't the equipment."

His green eyes traveled down her body leisurely and returned to her face. "You don't appear to be lacking any equipment to me," he said mildly.

Linda flushed to the roots of her hair. She would have liked to cut him down a peg or two for making that chauvinistic remark, but she knew her thoughtless statement had given him his opening.

"I meant the classy accent, the custom-made clothes, the aura of Beacon Hill." She smiled to take the sting out of her words.

He grinned suddenly, and Linda had to drop her eyes. She was drawn to him in spite of herself. Damn, she thought, he *was* attractive.

"Why madam, are you accusing me of using snob appeal to impress the masses?"

Linda raised her hand as if to ward off argument. "If the shoe fits..."

He was still smiling. "That is a remarkable statement, coming from you. How many times have I seen you flash those lovely legs, or use your limpid blue eyes to advantage in an impassioned plea? Come now, counselor, we all use the tools that nature has provided."

Linda watched as he turned toward her. His clean profile was limned in shadow. "Touché. But in the case of most of us, nature has not provided quite so much." She resented his ability to score points off her as well as he did with the witnesses in court, and as a result her remark had more bite to it than she had intended.

His smile faded when he realized his attempt to treat the subject lightly had failed. He eyed her intently for a moment.

"I'm sorry if I've offended you, Ms. Redfield," he said softly, and walked away.

Linda stood still, vaguely uncomfortable. He had been polite, even friendly, and she had acted like an ill-mannered brat. She felt that in some undefined way he had gotten the best of her again. Then she shook off her uneasiness and went to look for Maggie, pushing through the midday crowd milling about in the stone-floored lobby. Linda found her lounging on one of the side benches, and they walked to the entrance together, waving at the

Trial By Fire 5

guard who was examining the contents of satchels at the checkpoint. He nodded as they passed—he knew them and never stopped them. They passed through the revolving doors into the brilliant October day.

It was early fall in New England, and the leaves were just turning, confirming the hint of crispness in the air. The glory of the weather was lost on Linda, who was distracted as she fell into step beside Maggie.

"Let's go to the Oak Room and splurge," Maggie said. "We'll have wine and get drunk. What do you say?"

Linda appreciated Maggie's efforts, and walked with her up State Street to Main. By the time they reached the restaurant, the center dining room was almost full, and they were seated just as a line began to form.

Linda looked up from her menu to see Jefferson Langford three tables away with a stunning blonde. She groaned inwardly and looked down, but not before he had seen her and nodded.

"His majesty just acknowledged your presence." There wasn't much that got past Maggie.

"Should I have genuflected?" Linda responded.

Maggie giggled, then sobered uncharacteristically. "You know, we're not being very fair. I've heard from people who should know that he is not only a crackerjack lawyer but also a nice guy."

Linda was quite sure of the former, and she had an unwanted suspicion of the latter from her brief conversation with him. Hearing it confirmed didn't make her feel any better. "Who's that with him?"

Maggie rolled her eyes. *"That* is Diana Augusta Northrup, late of Bryn Mawr, resident of Philadelphia, Boston, and Bar Harbor. Can you imagine naming your daughter Diana Augusta? It must take three generations of blue blood just to get up the nerve." Maggie took a sip of her ice water. "Anyway, rumor has it that she is his intended."

Linda studied the neat pale coif, the peach silk shirt-dress, the perfect grooming of Langford's companion. "Intended for what? His display-window dummy? She looks as though a tornado wouldn't put a hair out of place."

Maggie laughed. "They seem right together, don't they?"

Linda felt a tug of the old resentment again. "Like a matched pair of pedigreed cocker spaniels."

Maggie met her gaze, and they both burst into laughter. From the corner of her eye Linda noticed Langford's head turn.

"Aren't we awful?" Maggie said. "I guess it's just jealousy. All that beauty and privilege together in one package. It seems unfair, somehow."

The waiter took their order, and Linda turned her chair slightly so she couldn't see the handsome couple. She'd had enough of Jefferson Langford for one day.

A week went by, with Linda caught up in her cases, working late several nights to do research and paper work. Langford faded from her mind, since she didn't see him in court and his firm was at the other end of State Street, near the courthouse and law library. The legal aid offices were in a converted storefront down-town, and she didn't normally travel in the same circles with Rolf, Langford, and Pinney, P.C.

So it came as a surprise to her when a distinguished white-haired gentleman in a pin-striped, three-piece suit stopped her in the hall outside the Domestic Relations court, where she had gone to file divorce papers for an indigent client. Linda stood in amazement as he asked her if he could have a moment of her time.

"I'd like to speak to you about a matter of mutual interest, Ms. Redfield," he said.

Linda was flattered that he knew who she was. She certainly knew him: Gordon Rolf, senior partner in Langford's father's firm, president of the County Bar Association, patron of the arts, barrister extraordinaire. She couldn't imagine what matter could be in their mutual interest.

"Shall we sit?" he suggested, gesturing toward the empty bench across the hall from them. Linda followed him and sat, intrigued.

"I've heard a number of good things about you, Ms. Redfield, from my partner's son, Jeff Langford. He tells me you're a fine young lawyer."

Linda was far too stunned to reply. After her behavior during her last conversation with Langford, she had expected him to obliterate her from his memory, or at the very least blacken her name if it ever came up. That he had complimented her to this pillar of the profession was not to be believed.

But Rolf was still talking. "And so when he needed to take on someone to help him with this case, he suggested you. It wouldn't be just for this one trial—we could arrange something permanent to your satisfaction, I'm sure."

Linda was transfixed, unable to absorb what she was hearing. Was he offering her a job?

Rolf misunderstood her hesitation. "I realize that it's a bit unusual to approach you in this manner, Ms. Redfield. I was going to telephone and arrange for a luncheon meeting with you and young Langford and myself, but when I saw you just now, I thought—"

"Oh, no," Linda blurted out, "that's quite all right." Was he kidding? He was offering her a chance of a lifetime and she wasn't about to object to his informality.

"How long do you think it will take to make up your mind?" he asked.

"May I let you know in a couple of days?" Linda said. She would have accepted on the spot but thought this pillar of the old school might find her ready acceptance indecent.

"Fine, fine," Rolf said, evidently pleased with the interview. "You'll need to give notice at your current position, but I think we can have you on board in short order if you decide to join us. Langford needs someone fairly quickly. Do you think two weeks' notice would be sufficient?"

This was all happening so fast that Linda felt dazed. One hour ago she had thought she would be a legal-aid attorney indefinitely, with no hope or chance for change, and now the senior partner in one of the oldest and most prestigious firms in the city was offering her a job. Her mind boggled.

"Two weeks would be plenty, I'm sure," she said, not knowing whether it would be. But she was certain that nothing was going to stand in her way of taking this job. Legal-aid attorneys were a dime a dozen. She would be replaced and forgotten almost overnight.

"Good. I'll tell Jeff I spoke with you, and we'll look forward to hearing from you soon."

Linda remained seated and watched as Rolf made his way down the corridor, stopping to talk to another senior member of the bar whom Linda had often seen in the courthouse. She couldn't wait to tell Maggie.

Maggie went into shock at the news. "Are you sure he said what you think he said?" she asked.

"I'm sure. He wants me to call him in a couple of days with my decision."

"He didn't discuss salary?"

"No. That's probably considered uncouth, or something. It's got to be more than I'm making here—anything would be. Besides, I don't care. What an opportunity! And I owe it all to Jefferson T. Langford III, boy wonder."

Maggie bit her lower lip thoughtfully. "Don't you find it a little strange that Langford asked for you on this job? I mean, he must know dozens of qualified people from better schools with more experience. Why you?"

Linda had asked herself the same question. "I don't know. But I'm certainly not going to waste time agonizing over it. Opportunity is knocking, and I'm going to yank open the door."

A slow smile was spreading over Maggie's face. "I can't wait to see the reaction here when you tell them you're leaving our lowly ranks to join Rolf, Langford, and Pinney. Perkins will drop his teeth."

Perkins was their supervisor, a career civil-service employee with the limited mentality often found in such types. "He'll probably think I'm blackmailing somebody."

"Or that you're Pinney's long-lost illegitimate daughter, brought up in a foundling home, returned to claim her rightful place at dear Daddy's side."

They laughed together, making up improbable explanations, each more outrageous than the last. But Linda could not quite rid herself of a nagging suspicion that she was setting herself up for more than just a new job.

Linda gave notice at Legal Aid and called Rolf to accept his offer. Then she went through the next couple of weeks in a tangle of mixed emotions. What if she couldn't handle this new position? She was making a quantum leap, and she wasn't sure she was ready for it.

She wasn't really as confident as she had pretended to Maggie. And what would it be like to work closely with Jefferson Langford on a daily basis? Though she told herself she didn't like him, there was something about him that disturbed her, made her feel insecure and juvenile. But she would have to try it and see, do her best to make it work.

She splurged on some new clothes, feeling rich on the new salary she would be getting, which was six thousand dollars more a year than Legal Aid had been paying her. Rolf had mentioned the figure rather casually during their phone conversation, saying that that was what they paid their beginning attorneys. It seemed like a fortune to Linda, who had already been working for two years. But she expected that she would earn it.

Chapter Two

LINDA DRESSED FOR the first day on the job in a tailor-made suit that had cost her a small fortune. She softened the effect of the fitted jacket and narrow skirt with a creamy jabot blouse and slender-heeled shoes. She brushed her black shoulder-length hair until it shone, and carefully applied her makeup. When she was done, she examined the effect in her full-length mirror. She saw the clear blue eyes, the pale skin, the curved figure and full mouth. She looked good. But she wasn't a Diana Northrup, she said to herself, and then was annoyed at the thought. She picked up her empty briefcase and marched to the car.

At Rolf, Langford, and Pinney, a secretary told her that Mr. Rolf had wanted to show her around himself, but that he had been detained. She was waved into an office down the hall. The whole floor was carpeted in gray plush, and the hushed but efficient atmosphere spoke of big doings behind closed doors. The receptionist answered the phone in dulcet tones that said money. Langford looked up as Linda walked through his door.

He motioned her to a chair, removing his tortoise-shell glasses and rubbing the bridge of his nose with his thumb and forefinger. He had obviously been reading for some time. Linda noticed that, unlike most people, glasses did not detract from his looks; they rather gave him the air of a charismatic young philosophy instructor at a junior college.

Langford regarded her levelly over a broad fruitwood desk. "We meet again, Ms. Redfield."

Linda nodded, not sure of what to say.

"I suppose Gordon told you I asked for you."

"Yes."

"And you were surprised."

"Yes."

He took a sip of coffee from a mug. He had discarded his jacket and club tie and opened several buttons on his shirt. Linda could see a clutch of dull bronze hairs at the vee, and hair of the same shade, darker than that on his head, on his forearms, where his sleeves were rolled to the elbows. He must look spectacular with a tan, she thought, and then came out of her reverie when he continued.

"I decided that there was some truth in what you said at our last meeting. Not much"—the ghost of a smile touched his lips—"but some. My grandfather founded this firm, and that's why I'm here. You are a good lawyer, as I have reason to know from being your opposition on several occasions. You had no chance to work for a firm like this because you had no connections, so I have provided the connection. In addition, we need a person for this case with contracts savvy, and as far as I can see you've done little else for two years but try to extricate your benighted clients from foolish agreements with landlords, loan companies, and retail stores. Is that correct?"

"That's correct."

He picked up a pencil and tapped the eraser against his teeth. "In my nine years of practice, I've found no better way to learn contracts than to construct a good defense."

His statement needed no response, so Linda merely waited, while rapidly calculating his age to be thirty-four.

His gaze shifted. "What's that you have in your hand?"

"My résumé. Mr. Rolf said to bring it to you."

"May I see it?"

He extended his hand, and Linda slapped the paper into it as if she were a surgical nurse handing over a scalpel. He sat back and scanned it.

"Mmm. American Jurisprudence Award in contracts. The highest grade in a class of how many?"

"Sixty-two."

His eyes widened. "I guess I was right about you."

Aren't you always right about everything? Linda wanted to say, but she held her tongue. It was amazing how this man managed to get under her skin. She had been grateful for the chance he was giving her and had been prepared to like him as a result, but after five minutes in his presence she could feel her irritation building. It wasn't anything in particular that he did. She simply couldn't explain it.

He continued to read. "Boston College," he said, naming her law school. "Very good."

"But not quite as good as Harvard," Linda said, her resolution to be agreeable forgotten in an instant.

He looked up sharply from the typewritten page and set it aside. He leaned back in his swivel chair and propped his ankle on his other knee, examining her thoughtfully.

"You don't like me much, do you, Ms. Redfield?"

Linda squirmed uncomfortably at this direct question. It was asked without malice but with the expectation of an honest reply.

"Why wouldn't I like you? I hardly know you."

"Exactly. You hardly know me, but it's clear you've formed a negative opinion of me." She started to say something, but he held up a hand. "You didn't answer my question—you evaded it—but I went to law school too, and I know what that means." He folded his arms on his chest and gazed at her coolly from eyes as green as bottle glass. "Shall I tell you what you think? Your parents were killed when you were twelve and you went to live with an aunt. You had to work your way through seven years of college with part-time and summer jobs. I, on the other hand, had everything you had to sweat for handed to me. You think I've come a long way on inherited money, family position, and superficial charm. How am I doing so far?"

While annoyed at the glibness of his speech, Linda had to admire the accuracy of his perception. Was she that transparent, or was he that clever? At any rate, since he had brought it up, she wasn't going to deny it. "A plus," she conceded.

"And now," he went on, "while you intend to make the most of this opportunity, and are prepared to tolerate me as part of the bargain, you covertly resent the fact that it took what you view as a handout from me to get you here."

Linda did not argue, meeting his challenging gaze directly.

He looked away, and sighed tiredly. "It's not a hand-out, Ms. Redfield. You deserve it."

Linda blinked at this. He sounded sincere.

"Well, you may not like me, but you're going to have

me, for the duration of this project, anyway." He paused. "Unless you want to ask Gordon to be reassigned. They're expanding the firm. I'm sure they'd take you on with my recommendation even if you didn't want to work on this case with me. I'll make up some plausible excuse."

Linda frowned, thoroughly puzzled. Why would he do that for her? She could understand his motivation in requesting her in order to get a competent assistant, which would make his job easier, but why would he suggest this alternative, which offered no benefit to himself? In any event, she wasn't going to begin this job by rocking the boat. She shook her head. "No, I'll stay with you."

"Don't want to bite the hand that feeds you, eh?"

Again he had read her thoughts with infuriating ease. She tried not bristle but her reaction must have shown, because he got up and walked around the desk. He sat on the edge of it, facing her, and leaned forward. He was so close she could see the tiny smattering of freckles on his nose, and in his eyes the rim of gold surrounding the pupil.

"Look," he said gently, "this is an important case for an important client. I'm going to be working closely with you for several months, and I want to do well with it. I'm willing to give you this chance because I think you're good and I think you can help me in this context. But I am not willing to watch every word I say for fear of upsetting your delicate sensibilities. Now, I want your word that you will put your personal feelings aside and dedicate yourself to this project, as I will, or I am going to get Gordon Rolf on the phone right now and have him assign you to another case."

Linda knew he meant it. "You have my word," she said firmly.

"Fine. Let's shake on it."

His grasp was hard and strong, his hand warm. As

he got up to go to his chair, he pushed back a lock of hair and murmured, "I must be out of my mind."

She knew what he was thinking. There were surely several dozen newly minted Ivy League lawyers who would jump at the chance he was giving her and lick his boots twenty-four hours a day in gratitude. He would regret his impulsive generosity quickly if she proved to be pain in the neck. She'd better lighten up and cooperate.

He sat again, putting papers into a large accordion file. "Now, down to business. In addition to Blackfoot, this firm represents several other large corporations. One of them, Puritan Petroleum, supplies fuel oil to many businesses and homes in the area, all of Western New England, in fact. The whole mess began when Puritan entered into a contract a year ago to supply oil to Springfield Tool at a certain price. Well, as you know, the cost of oil went up, and Puritan couldn't meet Springfield's demand at the agreed-upon price. The escalator clause, which provides for that, went into effect. And Springfield went elsewhere for its oil because they said Puritan violated the contract with an unfair price hike. The case itself is a simple, classic situation. The problem is that this contract has many contingencies. The person who drew it up has since been fired, but we are now stuck with interpreting what looks like the Bhagavad Gita in the original Sanskrit."

Linda pressed her lips together, amused.

"I spent two blinding hours reading it and the supporting material before you came in. I'm no better informed, but I now need a seeing-eye dog. This thing has been breached more often than the Indian treaties."

Linda stifled a smile. "By both sides?" she managed to ask.

"Oh, yes," he answered glumly. "They began carving it up like a Christmas turkey the moment they signed it."

Linda didn't laugh, but her grin was devilish. Langford looked up in time to see it, and stared.

"Why, Ms. Redfield, that's the first genuine smile I've seen from you. This is a momentous occasion—I must write it down in my diary." He tied the brown strings on the front of the envelope and handed it to her. "You won't think it's so funny a couple of days from now. Here you go. Have a ball. Let me be the first to know if you get any ideas. An office has been cleared for you across the hall. Take the rest of the day to familiarize yourself with the file. Then meet me here tomorrow at nine. We'll discuss it." He glanced at his watch. "I've got to be in court in twenty minutes."

"All right, Mr. Langford."

He paused on the threshold. "If we're going to be working together, don't you think we can dispense with this Mr. Langford, Ms. Redfield routine? We sound like a vaudeville act. I'm Jeff."

"And I'm Linda. Uh, Jeff?"

"Yes?"

"How did you know about my parents' death and my working my way through school? That information wasn't on my résumé."

He looked down at her, and the sunlight from his office window glinted on his bright hair. "You've been my adversary more than once. I always try to find out something about the person I'll be facing in a courtroom."

Together they walked out into the hallway, and Langford placed his hand on her arm. "Linda, one last thing," he said quietly. "Don't make assumptions about my background that may be unwarranted." He put his coat on and walked away, leaving her standing outside her office.

Linda found that her new clients were quite a departure from those she'd known at Legal Aid. Well dressed, soft-spoken, controlled, they came and went clothed in natural fibers and expensive scent, displaying breeding and civility like a patina of fine gold. Linda found, to her surprise, that she missed the Legal Aid clients. They might be scruffy, poor, abused, and sometimes abusive, but they were genuine. There was an air of insincerity about these lacquered denizens of the social register. They were refined, impressive, but almost too good to be true.

Her job was different from the old one in other ways too. The constant helpful presence of Mary, the secretary, both pleased and unnerved her. She wasn't used to being waited on. At Legal Aid, there had been one harried secretary, and she was usually so inundated with correspondence that she had little time for niceties. When Linda had asked where the photocopy machine was, and Langford had told her to just drop the material in the wire basket labeled "Xerox," it came as a surprise. But she soon realized that this was just one of many little services that were now performed for her. Coffee was served, letters transcribed, phone calls made, messages taken. In short, every effort was directed at leaving her free to work with Jeff—the biggest problem of her new situation.

Linda was honest in her assessment of the matter: she was very attracted to him. Who wouldn't be? His combination of looks, charm, and intelligence was a triple threat and difficult to resist. But she knew that other women probably reacted to him in the same way, and she wasn't about to jeopardize their professional relationship with so much at stake. So she carefully remained aloof, and on occasion she caught a fleeting, puzzled look in his depthless eyes, as if he could not fathom her attitude. Linda took a grim satisfaction in

this. Of course he couldn't understand it—he was used
to women dropping in their tracks if he so much as
glanced their way. Well, not this woman.

And so it went. They worked together, comparing
notes, sharing research, compiling cases to support their
position. She discovered that he had a keen legal mind,
plus a dry sense of humor that enlivened their sessions.
The better Linda got to know Langford, the more alluring
he became. She found it difficult to hold onto both her
initial impression of him and her studied detachment.

One day about a month after she had begun working
for the firm, Jeff stopped by her office at noon. This was
unusual, since usually he disappeared at midday with
Diana, resurfacing precisely an hour later. Linda wondered to what she owed the honor of the visit. Perhaps
Diana was having her hair done.

Langford dropped gracefully into one of her conference chairs and surveyed her with disturbing intensity.
Despite the fact that their working relationship had been
all business, Linda sometimes had the unexplainable feeling that the arrangement bothered him. This was one of
those moments.

He was wearing tan wool slacks with a cream linen
shirt and Welsh tweed jacket that highlighted his hair
and the gold flecks in his eyes. Linda sighed inwardly.
He was an attractive man completely at ease with himself.
The golden hair, fine features, and elegant form, how
was it possible that he took all that for granted? And yet
he seemed to.

"I was wondering how you felt you were working out
here," he began.

"That's for you to say, isn't it?"

"Not necessarily," he said quietly. "Are you being
treated well? Are you happy?"

What was this leading to? she wondered. "Of course."

"And me?" he persisted. "Do you feel comfortable working with me?"

Comfortable was not exactly the word for what she felt, Linda thought, but aloud she said, "You've been fair."

A wry smile touched his lips. "Fair?" He gave a snort of mirthless laughter. "Ah, Ms. Redfield, I fear you will never be the president of my fan club."

"Don't worry, Mr. Langford, I'm sure there are plenty of other candidates for that position. One less won't matter," she responded, unable to keep the sharpness out of her tone.

He blinked, then stood abruptly. "Dear lady, you disappoint me. Here, all this time, I've been thinking I was winning you over with my engaging wit and personality," he said with mild sarcasm, "but I see that the status is still quo." He straightened his tie and glanced at his watch. "I'm going to lunch. I'll meet you at one thirty to go over those Pennsylvania cases."

Puzzled, Linda watched him go through the door.

That had been a strange conversation. Why should he care whether he'd won her over or not? She could only conclude that her supposition had been correct; he was so accustomed to admiration that her one exception nagged him. She closed the hornbook on her desk with resignation. The riddle of Jefferson T. Langford would not be solved today.

Chapter Three

LINDA HAD BEEN concerned that Jeff's attitude toward her would change after their last confrontation. But when she saw him again he accorded her the same amiability with which he treated everyone. He seemed to have forgotten the incident, and so she behaved no differently. But she hadn't forgotten. She kept seeing the look on his face when she'd told him he'd been "fair," damning him with faint praise. It made her feel guilty.

The firm represented the Public Library Association in Longmeadow, and Linda had been assigned a case that required her to interview the library's curator. They had been unable to agree upon a time during the week, so on Saturday morning she went to meet him at his office. The library was in an old, converted mansion on the center green that had been donated to the town when its last heir died. Mr. Fairbairn's office was in the gatehouse behind the main building, and Linda looked forward to seeing the preserved 1700's structure, which was the subject of much rhapsodizing in the literature about the estate.

The autumn day was perfect. Longmeadow was always beautiful, but it was at its best in the fall, when the foliage burst forth in a dying blaze of glory. The restored houses fronting the mall sported red stars on the front, which indicated the Historical Society had marked them for funding. Each one had a plaque declaring the name of the first owner and the year it was built. "Ezekiel Hobson, 1679," Linda read aloud, driving slowly past a white saltbox with green shutters. The house bearing a plaque inscribed "Jeremiah Southwark, 1712" was a two-story clapboard affair with a wide front walk. How strange, and how sad, to think that the builders of these houses had been dust for centuries, while their handiwork survived them to the present day.

The fresh morning air was crisp and cool, and Linda rolled down her window. As she cruised by a small cream-colored Cape Cod-style house with a deep front lawn, the door opened, and Jeff walked out onto the porch.

Linda was so surprised that she almost jammed on the brakes. She knew he lived in Longmeadow, but she had assumed his home was in one of the luxury condominiums in the newer part of the borough.

There was no mistaking his slim, erect figure or bright hair. She halted at a stop sign and watched him in the rearview mirror. He wore loose navy track pants that tied at the waist, and a hooded, zip-front gray sweatshirt. For a few moments he danced around at the top of the steps, like a boxer preparing for the ring. The driver behind Linda blew his horn, and she drove on as Jeff trotted lightly down the stairs and fell into a steady jogging pace along the street.

Linda's reaction to the unexpected sight of him was

abrupt and violent. She shook her head. You've got it bad, she mumbled to herself. She pulled into the library parking lot on the other side of the street and extracted the curator's card from her wallet. Her appointment was for nine thirty, not nine o'clock. She was forty minutes early. Since it was Saturday, the library was still closed, so she couldn't pass the time reading. Damn. Annoyed with herself, she tapped her fingernails on the steering wheel restlessly.

She had to admit that there was another reason for her discomfiture. Seeing Jeff running like that had reminded her of Jim. Though she managed to put him out of her thoughts quite successfully under normal circumstances, it was the unexpected jolts to the memory that sent a surge of pain through her like heat lightning in a summer sky.

She had met Jim when she was a senior in college, and married him in a rosy glow of physical passion that soon dissipated in the harsh light of reality. He had worked in his father's construction business. Big and bluff and handsome, he was a typical macho man, and Linda had not examined the consequences of his attitudes until she had to deal with them on a day-to-day basis. After they were married, he had wanted her to quit school. Since he was going to support her always, there was no need for her to further her education. Their argument over that issue was the first of many. Linda continued to take classes at night, telling him that they were in cooking and macrame—of which he approved. And this decep-tion, when revealed, caused a rift that nothing could mend. She had paid for the courses with money she had saved, and this was another blow to his pride. When she managed to get her degree, he wanted her to stay home and have children, while Linda had wanted to use her diploma as a springboard to a career. By the time she graduated, the marriage was in deep trouble.

That spring she went secretly to job interviews, praying that somehow she could get him to accept the situation once she had a firm job offer. As it turned out, her fears were unwarranted. Jim was killed one May day, when the scoop of an earth mover caught him in the back of the head as he walked backwards along the edge of a ditch.

They had been married less than a year, but the guilt over her relationship with him took a lot longer to resolve. Linda knew she had not made him happy, and the bitterness of his family, especially his mother, wounded her deeply. Mrs. Redfield couldn't understand this strange girl with the newfangled ideas about college and careers. Why couldn't she just let Jimmy take over, as she had let his father? All he wanted to do was be good to her. There were thousands of girls in the country who would thank God for someone like her son to solve their problems. She had said as much to Linda at every opportunity. When Jim died, the family washed their hands of her. They had been barely civil to Linda at the funeral, arriving at her home the same day to pack Jim's personal effects. The house had been in both their names, so Linda had sold it and used the money to buy the townhouse in Springfield where she now lived. She had given the furniture to Goodwill, not wanting a reminder of an unhappy chapter in her life. Then she had taught English for a year, and started law school the following fall.

Now, with the perspective of six years to balance her evaluation, Linda was sure she had not been wrong. All she had wanted was what many women today wanted. During the time since Jim's death she had met lots of men whose wives had dynamic, interesting careers, and their husbands weren't threatened by them. She had merely picked the wrong man to share her vision. So she had made her peace with her memories. But the sight of Jeff in the navy pants and gray top had touched a sensitive nerve. Jim had loved to run. He used to get up early in the morning before work to do it, in an outfit very similar to the one Jeff was wearing now.

The thought of Jeff brought her mind back to the present. When he had recounted her life history on her first day with the firm, he had made no mention of her brief marriage. Did he know about it? she wondered. For some uncertain reason, this bothered her.

She glanced at her watch. It was 8:53 A.M. She felt ridiculous, sitting in her car indulging in counterproductive ramblings on the past. Then she had an idea. Feeling like a voyeur, she inched the car back out onto the green and drove along until she caught sight of Jeff running in the distance. Keeping some distance behind him, she followed him as he made his way through town toward Springfield. She watched him abruptly turn at the corner store, and she pulled behind the real estate office across the street.

Moments later he came out holding a cardboard container of juice. He dropped on the tree-shaded bench by the side of the road and held the obviously cold waxy cylinder against his forehead. She watched secretly as he pulled off the top and took a healthy slug. His legs were splayed out before him. He threw his head back and draped his arms along the top of the bench, resting.

Traffic passed as Linda waited, fascinated. Finally he stood and stripped off the pants and sweatshirt, using them to towel his thighs and midriff. Underneath he was wearing a faded T-shirt emblazoned with Harvard's motto "Veritas," or "Truth," and equally well-worn notched shorts. He made a pillow of the clothes in the hood of the shirt and tied the arms around his neck. Finishing his drink, he discarded the box in a wire litter basket next to the bench. He propped first one leg, then the other, on the seat of the bench and kneaded the muscles between knee and ankle.

Linda was aware of how much he intrigued her, if watching him in this mundane activity gave her such a thrill. When he started running again she followed him out. She trailed him almost as far as the library and was preparing to turn off, when Jeff pulled up short and dropped to the pavement as if he'd been shot.

Linda forgot her resolution to remain undetected. She gunned the motor and pulled up alongside the walkway, where Jeff sat hunched over, with his knees to his chest, grimacing. When he looked up and saw her, his eyes widened with astonishment.

"Linda, what are you doing here?" he asked, attempting to stand but unable to do so. The muscles in the lower part of his left leg twitched wildly. Sweat stood out on his forehead, and he closed his eyes against the pain.

"I have an appointment in town and happened to be driving by," she said, which was only half a lie. "I saw you fall. Let me help you."

Linda helped him to his feet, and he draped his arm around her shoulders. He hobbled to her car and collapsed in the passenger seat, drawing up the injured leg and rubbing it fiercely.

"Where's your place?" Linda asked, pretending ignorance. He pointed wordlessly, and she pulled into the gravel driveway. Over his protests she ran around to his side and helped him out, supporting him as they went up the steps. She was conscious of his heated body, the heady male scent of perspiration. He indicated a chaise longue on the enclosed front porch, and she eased him onto it. He bent to rub the leg again, and Linda pushed his hands away.

"Let me do it," she said, kneeling next to him. "I

used to play basketball in high school. I've handled this kind of thing before."

He looked at her for a moment, but he was too wrung out to protest. He let his head drop back on the cushion as she kneaded the knotted calf muscles, which were as tight as bowstrings. His breathing slowed, and she could see him relaxing as the cramp eased.

"It's better now," he said.

"That was a calf splint."

"Calf splint? Whatever you say, Florence Nightingale."

"Do you know why it happened?" Linda asked, continuing to manipulate his flesh, noting his lean body-fat and the big, powerful veins of the hard-working runner.

"Calcium deficiency," he said through his teeth as she felt the muscle beneath her hands tighten again. "I've been swallowing the pills, drinking milk, everything, but I guess it wasn't enough. I've had minor spasms before, but this was definitely the grand kahuna."

"What does your doctor say?" she queried, loath to stop touching him.

Jeff winced and gripped the side arms of the chaise when she applied more pressure. "He says to stop running."

"Then why don't you?"

"If I stop running," he stated, "I will turn into a hideous mass of blubber overnight."

Linda laughed shortly. "That's absurd."

He shrugged. "I'm not going to wait for it to happen to prove my point." He watched her fingers at work. "I'm glad you came along. If you hadn't, I'd probably still be out there on the sidewalk, whimpering like a beggar."

"Oh, I daresay someone would have come along," Linda replied. Probably another female, she added silently, thinking of the picture he had made, his athlete's body stretched on the pavement.

His eyes slitted pleasurably as the crisis passed. His mouth curved into the beginnings of a sly smile. "Uh, I think my thigh is a little cramped too," he said innocently.

Linda dropped his leg. "I think you're fine."

"Aw, shucks." He grinned.

Linda stood and caught sight of a clock in the room beyond the door. "Oh, my gosh, I'm late for my appointment. I'd better call. May I use your phone?"

"It's in the hall," he directed, standing gingerly and examining his leg suspiciously, as if it were about to cripple him once more. She found the phone on a small desk in the entry and telephoned Mr. Fairbairn, pleading car trouble as an excuse. He said he could see her at eleven, so she had a free hour.

"Everything okay?" Jeff asked when she found him in the kitchen, making coffee.

"We rescheduled it for eleven."

"Good. Then you can have a cup of coffee with me to celebrate my recovery." He removed a half-gallon container of milk from the refrigerator and poured a large glass of it. "I feel like an expectant mother," he said, draining every drop. "Doesn't seem to be doing a bit of good anyway." He looked at her standing in the doorway. "How about a tour of my domain?"

She nodded.

"Limp after me," he said. He stopped in the doorway and gestured back at the room. "This, as you can tell, is the kitchen. It was the cookhouse/smokehouse when old Jason Turnbull built the place in 1772, and has been remodeled several hundred times since. I left the old oven and pot-bellied stove. Do you think they're nice touches?"

Linda looked around at the modern tiled floor and the

brightly painted yellow cabinets, with the big window open to the backyard letting sunshine in to wash the room. Old and new blended charmingly. "It's lovely."

He smiled at her. "I'm glad you think so." She followed him down the narrow hall to the living room, which was furnished sparingly with obviously valuable antiques. "I brought a few things from home," he said casually.

He had converted one of the two first-floor bedrooms into a study, piled high with law books, files, and papers. "This is what is laughingly known as my den," he said. "The President is about to declare it a national disaster area. I'm waiting for the federal funds to begin reclamation work."

The other first-floor bedroom had a television and an elaborate stereo system placed in a wall of shelves. "The master and guest bedrooms are upstairs," he said. "I'd take you up there, but I think the shock might cause you permanent damage. My cleaning lady is due this afternoon, and her services are sorely needed."

"Don't be so sure the mess would throw me," Linda replied. "In college, my dorm room had a sign over the door: 'Abandon all hope, you who enter!'"

Jeff laughed, and Linda glowed at his appreciation of her joke. The coffee was ready when they got back to the kitchen, and he poured it into earthenware mugs.

Linda was fascinated by this insight into his private life. It told her that even with his money, he preferred to live in genial semiconfusion in this little house, rather than in the glass-and-chromium splendor one might have imagined.

"Why did you buy this place?" Linda asked curiously. "Weren't you tempted by those color-coordinated decorator's delights, all austere neutrals and potted ferns?"

He paused to look at her, a mug in each hand. "Did you think I might be?" he asked, as though disappointed by her misjudgment of him.

"Obviously not," she said, avoiding a direct reply.

He sat across from her at the maple drop-leaf table. "I bought the place because I liked it," he said simply. "It was the right size and location, and this section of town is beautiful. I love old houses. You can imagine the generations living here, making love, giving birth. Happy families," he added, almost wistfully. Then he looked up quickly and caught her staring at him. "You know."

"Yes, I know what you mean."

"When the real estate agent brought me here, the place sort of spoke to me. I've been here for five years."

Linda gazed at him. In his track shorts and T-shirt, with his strawberry-blond hair mussed and matted from exertion, he looked like a fourth grader enthusiastically discussing his new train set. Linda felt a rush of affection and warmth so strong that she was sure it showed on her face. To cover it, she stood, smoothing the wrinkles from her skirt.

"I have to go, Jeff. I don't want to be late again."

He walked her to the front of the house and held the door open for her. "Thanks for the rescue, though somehow I think it's supposed to be the other way around. I'm supposed to aid the damsel in distress."

"Wrong century, counselor. Rescues work both ways nowadays."

As she started to go down the steps, his voice stopped her. "Where's your appointment?"

"At the library with Mr. Fairbairn."

"That's right across the street. Why don't you come back here when you're through, and we'll get started on those Second Circuit cases? I brought all the material home. We might as well do it together and not duplicate our efforts."

This made perfect sense. She had planned on spending the weekend by herself doing the very same thing. She could certainly use his experience and guidance. But the idea bothered her. Working alone with him at his house was not exactly the same as working with him at the office.

But Linda did not want him to know that she was attaching any particular significance to his offer. He was merely trying to be nice and get the work done at the same time. He'd think her a ninny if she acted skittish at such a perfectly innocuous suggestion. There was really no reasonable objection she could make. She had already told him yesterday that she would be holed up with the Second Circuit until Monday morning. If she invented some errand or social engagement now, he'd know she was lying.

"All right, Jeff. I don't know how long I'll be with Mr. Fairbairn, but I'll come back here when I'm through."

"Great. See you then." He went back inside the house, leaving Linda to figure out how to dispense with Mr. Fairbairn as quickly as possible.

Mr. Fairbairn's office proved to be everything the literature said it was, but Linda was in no mood to appreciate it. His problem was a minor tax discrepancy, and not very demanding. She had the impression that the firm humored him as a sop to his son-in-law, the mayor. She did her best for the old man and was back at Jeff's door at two o'clock. Even so, the interview took longer than she had hoped to, since she wound up having lunch with Mr. Fairbairn and a couple of his committee members. She realized she had been a distracted guest; twice she had been expected to respond to a comment she hadn't heard. When she finally left, her exit was more like a flight than a departure.

She knocked on Jeff's front door, and heard him calling from within. "Is that you, Linda?"

"Yes."

"Come in, it's open."

She found him sitting cross-legged on the kitchen floor, wearing a T-shirt, brown corduroy cut-offs, and leather top-siders. A disassembled toaster was perched in his lap, with the parts scattered all around him on the tiles.

"Hi," he said. "How'd it go?"

"Oh, fine. The library has some quibble about its tax-exempt status. It shouldn't be too much of a hassle."

"Good. If you need any help with it, see Craig Jensen at the firm. He handles all the major tax work. I'll introduce you to him."

"Thanks. What are you doing?"

"I am attempting to repair this monument to modern science. It throws off sparks every time I plug it in. One of these days it's going to short-circuit me and half of Longmeadow."

"What's wrong with it?"

"That's what I'm trying, and failing, to find out. Seven years of college, and I can't fix a toaster. What does it mean?"

"It means you're a lawyer, not an appliance repairman."

He held up a GE manual. "When all else fails, read the directions." He struggled with it a few moments longer, and then dumped everything into a cardboard box and shoved it under the sink. "Maybe a magic word will come to me in a dream," he muttered.

Linda smiled. "I guess you're just not mechanically inclined."

"That's putting it mildly. I bought my car because *Consumer Reports* said that it had the best track record for repairs. I hope so, because if I'm ever called upon to do anything for it, I'll be reduced to the most primitive form of transportation—my feet. I try to take care of it, but I'm still convinced it's going to collapse all at once into a heap of rubble."

Linda laughed, wondering what had happened to the suave, aloof barrister she'd seen so often in court. At home he was completely different, like a chameleon who had discarded protective coloration.

They heard a series of thumps from above, and Jeff closed his eyes. "That's Mrs. Costik, reconstructing my bedroom. Now she's going to come down here and yell at me."

As if on cue, an overweight gray-haired woman in her sixties lumbered heavily down the stairs, catching sight of Jeff in the kitchen. She pounced on him, a small terry-cloth bundle in her hand.

"Mr. Langford, what is this?"

"Mrs. Costik, that is a towel," he answered dutifully.

"What was it doing under your bed?"

He stared at the housekeeper, his eyes wide and guileless. "I can't imagine, unless..." He narrowed his eyes sternly, folding his arms on his chest. "Have you been putting towels under my bed again, Mrs. Costik?"

"Everybody's a comedian," she said humorlessly, noticing Linda. "Who's this?"

"This, Mrs. Costik, is a colleague of mine from the office, another attorney, Ms. Linda Redfield."

"A lawyer?" Mrs. Costik asked, peering at Linda.

"That's right. And you'd better not ask her why she isn't staying home knitting afghans and having Tupperware parties, or she'll turn into Susan B. Anthony right before your very eyes."

"Who's Susan B. Anthony?" Mrs. Costik replied.

Jeff slapped his cheek in mock horror. "Blasphemy! Asking Ms. Redfield that is like asking a cultist who Krishna is."

Mrs. Costik ignored him and directed her remarks to Linda. "Do you know what he's talking about? I never know what he's talking about. Have you had lunch?"

"Yes."

"And I don't have to ask you that question," she said to Jeff. "What keeps you going, I'll never know." She surveyed him critically, frowning. "How tall are you, Mr. Langford?"

"I'm six feet two inches tall, Mrs. Costik."

"And how much do you weigh?"

"I weigh one hundred eighty-three pounds, Mrs. Costik."

"Well, there you go. My Billy is the same height and he tops that by fifty pounds."

"Her Billy is a lumberjack in Oregon," Jeff explained, miming the outline of a gorilla behind Mrs. Costik's back.

"You can stop making those faces," she said to Jeff, not even turning around. "At least Billy knows enough to eat a decent meal once in a while." She walked over to a pantry built into one wall and yanked the door open. *"That* is what *he* lives on," she told Linda, pointing to the shelves, which contained several boxes of individually packaged instant breakfast in assorted flavors.

"They're very well balanced," Jeff said to Linda. "Read the label."

"Look at this," Mrs. Costik went on, opening the refrigerator and gesturing at the contents like a magician's assistant revealing a marvel. Linda saw half a dried-up lemon, a jar of pickles, and three gallons of milk. That's for the instant breakfast and the calcium deficiency, she thought, smiling. "Now, I ask you," Mrs. Costik went on, not amused, "is that any way for a grown man to live?"

"Oh, leave her alone, Mrs. Costik. You've just met her, and already you're enlisting her in your crusade to reform my dietary habits. I promise you, I am not going to drop dead from malnutrition."

The interchange was interrupted by a fierce scratching at the door that led to the backyard. Jeff opened it, and a large mongrel dog jumped up his legs in a frenzy of joy. Jeff got down on his knees and let the dog lick his face.

"Nathan," he exclaimed, digging his fingers into the wealth of coarse hair at the scruff of the animal's neck, "you old rattlesnake. I didn't see you for a few days. I was afraid you had migrated south for the winter."

"And that's another thing," Mrs. Costik said, as if continuing the same conversation, "that dog is a disgrace. If it is a dog. It looks like a wolf to me."

"A chihuahua looks like a wolf to you," Jeff said to Mrs. Costik. He turned to Linda. "I brought home a little puppy and, size-wise, it has turned into the Hound of the Baskervilles."

"Tell the girl the truth," Mrs. Costik said. She turned to Linda. "One freezing night last January, he found the pup abandoned at the town dump, and of course it wound up here. It sheds all over the furniture and drags filthy bones through the house. Don't ask me what Mr. Know-It-All was doing at the dump—I don't inquire about those things."

Linda was beginning to feel like the referee at a debate.

"Naturally I brought him home. What could I do? He

adopted me," Jeff defended himself. "And I was at the dump to check out the depth of the landfill for a case. She makes it sound as if I were there to pick through the garbage."

Linda laughed.

"His name is Nathan," Jeff said. "Justice Benjamin Nathan Cardozo, actually. Nate to his friends. I was going to call him Benjy, but a movie star claimed it first."

Linda petted the dog's large, multicolored head. "How do you do, Justice Cardozo? You don't look anything like your pictures."

The dog shambled into the kitchen and sat before a low cabinet, staring at it fixedly. Then he threw back his head and howled.

Mrs. Costik spread her hands. "A wolf, I told you."

"He's just hungry, aren't you, boy?" Jeff said. He opened a cabinet, to reveal about fifteen cans of dog food. "How about beef and liver stew? Sound good?" He opened a can and dished out the dinner for the dog.

"Sure," Mrs. Costik said. "Food for himself, no. Food for the dog, yes." She trundled off, announcing loudly over her shoulder that she was going to do the laundry and would be down in the cellar.

Jeff wiped imaginary moisture off his forehead. "Whew! I got off easily today. Last week she found a tuna sandwich with one bite out of it in the trash bin. I thought she was going to beat me up."

Linda found his obvious fondness for the querulous housekeeper and the stray dog a striking contrast to the impression she'd always had of him. Was he really this . . . endearing?

Jeff led the way to his den, where he had cleared a space for them to work amidst the chaos. Nate followed, jumping onto a blanket that was obviously his, on the seat of a leather chair. Curling into a ball, he promptly went to sleep.

Jeff had photocopied and stapled the pages of each case together, underlining the pertinent parts in red. Linda was amused to see that he had developed the universal fondness of the law student for the felt marker: with so much reading to do, it was virtually impossible to keep up without highlighting the material for easier identification later. Otherwise, one had to pore over useless material at random to locate what was needed. Linda's own books and notes were underscored and drawn through in the same way. For some reason, this idiotic detail delighted her. He was human, after all.

They each took a stack and got started, outlining the major points of each case on index cards. Time passed as they worked in companionable silence. Her awareness of the man in the room with her was so acute that Linda had difficulty concentrating on what she was doing.

He was sitting with his feet propped on a hassock, the papers he was reading in his lap, pen and note cards on a side table. Whenever he came across something of interest, he would mark it in the margin and rapidly scrawl a few lines on a card. A shaft of late-afternoon sunlight set fire to his hair and cast deep shadows along the planes of his face. Linda could see the cleft between his collar bones where the shirt stopped, and had a very strong urge to trace it with the tip of her finger. Realizing that she was staring, she forced herself to turn back to her reading.

He finished his cases first and waited for her, rereading his notes until she was ready to confer with him. When she looked up, he said, "Okay. What have you got?"

They discussed their efforts, and came up with two

cases that looked promising enough to investigate further.

"So it's *Dexter* vs. *D'Amico Fuel Suppliers*, 412 U.S.136, and *Abernathy* vs. *Shamrock Petroleum*, 408 U.S. 65. Agreed?"

"Agreed."

"Fine. We'll go to the state and unofficial reporters on Monday and find out what the story was, from the lower courts on up." He stretched, and his shirt rode up to expose a spare, muscular belly above the low-riding jeans. Linda felt a surge of desire so strong that she had to look away. Oblivious, Jeff stood, arching back from the waist to loosen a kink from sitting in the same position for so long.

"Time for a little something," he said. "Let's see. I can offer you instant breakfast, dog food, or more coffee. Which will it be?"

"I'll take the coffee."

"Somehow, I thought you would," he said, grinning engagingly. "However, with the foresight for which I am known throughout New England, I sent out to the grocery store when I knew you would be coming back later this afternoon. They should have left a little surprise package on the porch by now, along with an even more surprising bill. Every time I sneeze, their prices go up."

"You shouldn't have gone to the trouble."

"Hey, forget it. Nate and I enjoy the chance to play host. We usually tough it out alone on the weekends, so this is an event. Twice in one day, too. Wait until Mrs. Costik sees the nourishing food I ordered. She'll shed real tears."

He went out to fetch the snack, followed by Nate, and Linda went to examine the other bedroom in his absence. Its contents showed that he had liberal tastes in both literature and music. The books ranged from best-selling fiction to natural science and biography, while the records and tapes covered all ranges from Beethoven to the Beatles. Linda was reacquainting herself with one album when Mrs. Costik bustled by on her way out.

"I'm leaving now, miss. I told Mr. Langford that the laundry's all dried and folded downstairs, but he forgets, so remind him, will you? He'll be calling me tomorrow, asking me where his track shorts are." She sighed, then looked Linda over closely. "He's out in the kitchen now, putting away that mountain of food he ordered. I'd like to see you come here every day, miss, if it would get that one to keep some decent supplies in his house." She waved goodbye and left without further comment.

When Jeff came in a few minutes later, carrying a tray, Linda was conscious that they were now alone in the house.

"I think he likes you," Linda said, indicating the dog, who was at his heels.

Jeff smiled. "He reminds me of that poem, 'I have a little shadow that goes in and out with me.'"

"'And what can be the use of him is more than I can see,'" Linda finished the line.

"That part doesn't apply," Jeff said, pouring the coffee. "I have these biscuits here," he said self-consciously. "I asked the clerk what one would serve to a lovely young lady for afternoon tea, and she suggested these. They're probably what old ladies munch on while discussing the failings of their various relatives, but this is the best I could do on short notice."

Undone by his ingenuousness, Linda took a cookie in silence, not sure what to say. They were good, not too sweet, an English brand she had seen in specialty and gourmet shops.

"Mrs. Costik thought she was having a vision when she saw me putting away the frozen vegetables," he said, mischief in his voice. "I told her it was all due to your good influence, and I think it's accurate to say you have a friend for life."

"She's very devoted to you," Linda said. "Like a second mother."

"Like a first," Jeff said, in a tone that made Linda hesitate to ask him what he meant. However, before she could, he changed the subject.

"You mentioned earlier that you used to play basketball," he said.

"Years ago, in high school," she confirmed.

"Well, once a year we run a benefit day for the children's wing at Johnson Memorial. It's coming up in a couple of weeks. It's a game between a team from the firm and a team from the pediatric clinic at the hospital. The bar association and the hospital both support it. We play at the YMCA downtown," he added. "The families and friends come to see us make fools of ourselves, and we usually raise a good chunk of money for equipment and research and so on. There's a bonfire and a Halloween costume party at night. Will you be on the team?"

"Jeff, I haven't played in eight years. I'd cross the midline once and have a cardiac arrest," she said, surprised at his request.

"I doubt that. You look pretty nimble to me. Come on, what do you say? We always have trouble getting women to play. The hospital outdoes us every year with all the nurses."

Linda found that she couldn't say no to him, even though the prospect of playing in front of a group filled her with dread.

"All right," she finally agreed. "But don't expect much."

"It's nothing to worry about," he said reassuringly. "You won't be playing that long in any case. We usually field about fifteen, and make a lot of substitutions."

That was easy enough to understand. There were thirty-two lawyers on staff at the firm, and that did not include support personnel as a source of athletic material. Linda hoped there were a lot of interested, talented amateur basketball players available this year, because she wanted her participation to be as limited as possible.

They went back to work on another segment of the project, and the telephone rang at about six-thirty. Linda was amazed how much time had passed; she felt as if she had just arrived.

Jeff got up to answer the phone, while Linda continued reading, not paying much attention until his voice spoke a familiar name.

"I know I said eight o'clock, Diana."

Of course, it was Saturday night, and he had a date. Linda came down off the cloud she had been on all afternoon with a crash. No matter how well they got along as far as work went, there was no question where Jeff's real, and permanent, interest lay. In a way it was good that Linda overheard what she had. There was nothing like a large dose of reality to keep the fantasies at bay.

Linda started gathering her things together before Jeff returned. She was not going to provide him with the task of trying to think of a tactful way of getting rid of her so he could get ready for his date.

"Jeff," she said when he came into the room, "I didn't realize how late it was. I'm going out tonight, and I've got to run."

He actually seemed disappointed. Was it her imagination? Hadn't she just heard him say he was booked for eight o'clock? Well, no matter. She didn't need a brick to fall on her head. He was Diana's territory, and their afternoon together was just a brief friendly interlude.

In her haste to be gone, Linda tripped over the partially exposed cord of a lamp. The impetus of her fall pitched her forward, and Jeff leaped to catch her in midair.

He hugged her close to steady her. The impact of his body was tremendous; she felt staggered, overwhelmed. He smelled of soap and starch, and that distinctly male scent was unmistakable. She could feel his shoulder blades beneath her fingers, the powerful muscles of his thighs pressing against her.

He cradled her close for a few seconds, then held her off, gazing down at her.

"Are you all right?" he asked.

Linda couldn't answer for the pounding of her heart. She merely stared back at him mutely. They looked into each other's eyes, sharing the magic, the fascination that was as new as their meeting, as old as the continents.

She saw his lips part, saw his face coming toward hers. His lashes were drifting downward as their mouths met.

Linda knew she should resist, but she found herself powerless to do so. He pulled her more tightly against him, and she wound her arms around his neck. His skin was warm, satiny to the touch. The little hairs at his nape were soft and silky. She let herself drift in a world of feeling.

He moved his head and kissed her throat, his lips tracing the path of her collarbone down inside the opening of her blouse. She arched to meet him. His hair, fragrant from shampoo, brushed her nostrils as he bent to caress her with his lips. She made a faint, involuntary sound of pleasure, but he heard it. He gathered her in his arms and led her to the sofa.

"Stay," he said, drawing her across his knees. "Stay with me." It was phrased like a command but sounded more like a plea.

Hearing him say it brought her to her senses. She struggled to a sitting position. "I can't," she gasped, pulling at her disordered clothes.

"Why not?" he murmured, reaching for her, still in the throes of their sudden burst of passion. A vein throbbed in his forehead, and his lips appeared raw. I must look the same, she thought wildly: drugged with sensation.

"You know why not," she said cryptically. There were any number of reasons, not least of which was his date in a couple of hours.

She stood unsteadily, avoiding his clinging hands. She refused to look at him. That would be madness.

He watched her as she prepared for flight. His breathing was ragged as she could see by the rise and fall of his chest. She wanted to run back to him, but forced herself in the opposite direction, toward the door.

"Goodbye, Jeff," she called desperately, trying to escape before he could stand to see her out.

As she pulled out of the driveway, she saw him behind the screen door, following her with solemn eyes.

Chapter Four

AFTER THAT SATURDAY at Jeff's house, Linda was more baffled by him than ever. She couldn't equate the boyish naif who didn't know what to serve for a coffee break in his own home with the cool antagonist she saw in court, with the cultured socialite who could order in flawless French at the most expensive restaurant in town. Which was he? Was he both? It seemed impossible to combine such diverse facets in one nature, but he apparently did.

Jeff introduced Linda to Craig Jensen on Monday, and he gave her excellent advice on the library's tax problem. He was a year or two older than Linda, a bespectacled, curly-haired whiz kid who was already acquiring a reputation for inventing creative solutions for the tax dilemmas of the firm's clients. Linda liked him immediately, and accepted his invitation to go out for a drink after work on Friday.

Craig selected a nearby pub that had a "happy hour"

from five to seven. The lounge was smoky and crowded, filled with work-weary employees eager to relax at the end of a long week. They found a small table at the back, and Linda ordered a drink, which she didn't want, so she sipped it sparingly, trying to get into the spirit of the place. The crush was unbelievable; Linda could hardly see through the cigarette haze.

Craig had been with the firm for a year and told anecdotes about it and his practice, which Linda found amusing until he sat back and surveyed her with a little half smile playing about his lips. "So, tell me, how do you like working with the golden boy?"

"Who?" she asked innocently.

Craig was not fooled. "Oh, you know, the heir-apparent. Jefferson Langford, Esquire."

"So far it's gone well, I think," Linda said noncommitally.

"You're not smitten? Not enchanted, like every other female in the place, from the lowliest stenographer to Pinney's wife?" He looked amazed. "You're a rare woman, Ms. Redfield."

"So I keep telling everyone."

Craig shook his head. "The grapevine also says that you're smart, capable, and, best of all, *humble*. The girl of my dreams. Will you marry me?"

Linda smiled. "Don't you think we should at least exchange phone numbers first?"

He grabbed a matchbook from the table and scribbled his number down. "Here's mine. Does this mean we're engaged?"

Linda laughed at his nonsense. Then he said, in a subdued tone, "Oh, speak of the devil. There's himself, with Lady Di in tow."

Linda looked up and saw Jeff and Diana moving

through the crowd. Jeff's eyes were on Linda.

"There goes my plan to get you alone and seduce you," Craig muttered. "They're coming over here."

Linda felt her pulse quicken as Jeff and Diana approached. Jeff was still in the clothes he'd worn to work, a black pin-striped suit with an off-white shirt and a brick-red tie. Diana glowed in a deep-salmon pants outfit shot through with gold thread and sporting a gold belt. She had probably met him after work to go to dinner, and they had stopped for drinks first.

Linda felt positively dowdy in the green-and-navy plaid skirt and the navy blazer she'd had on all day. Diana's neatness always made her feel as if she'd just stepped out of a wind tunnel. She smoothed her hair and quickly arranged her skirt over her knees. Oh, well.

Craig stood as Jeff introduced Diana to Linda. Diana smiled, displaying small, even teeth.

"I'm so happy to meet you, Linda," Diana said pleasantly. "Jeff has told me what an asset you are to the firm. He's been congratulating himself on hiring you since the day you began."

Linda searched the other woman's face for some sign of insincerity, but found none. Diana was simply being gracious to one of Jeff's colleagues, no more, no less.

They talked for a bit while Jeff and Craig discussed a case Linda knew nothing about. She was forced to admit that her judgement, based on Diana's appearance, might have been hasty. She really should grow up, she thought, and wait until she got to know people a little better before pigeonholing them.

Craig went back to the bar for another drink, and Diana was talking with someone she knew in the crowd. In the chattering throng Jeff and Linda found themselves in an oasis of silence.

Finally Jeff spoke. "Are you dating Craig now?"

"He asked me to join him for a drink after work," Linda said smoothly.

Jeff gazed back at her from deeply fringed, inscrutable eyes, and she wondered what he was thinking. Why should he be interested in Linda's social life, especially when he had Diana waiting to go out on the town with him?

Craig returned, and the uncomfortable moment passed. Diana rejoined them to say that she and Jeff had better get going, since they had a reservation. For just a moment Linda was afraid she might suggest that Linda and Craig join them. But they said goodbye and departed, Linda's eyes lingering on the twin heads until they were out of sight, swallowed up by the crowd.

"You know," Craig said thoughtfully, "the Aztecs used to pick the most physically perfect couple in the clan each planting season, and then sacrifice them for a plentiful rainfall and a bountiful harvest. I don't think those two would have lasted long, do you?"

Linda laughed in rueful agreement.

Craig tried to talk Linda into going out with him for dinner, but she pleaded fatigue, and they parted outside the pub. Linda's sleep that night was disturbed by restless dreams, but in the morning she could not remember them.

The next afternoon, Linda found Maggie waxing the kitchen floor of her apartment while listening to a PBS reporter interview a well-known celebrity.

"They told me if I went to law school I wouldn't have to do this anymore," Maggie said, upending her sponge mop in a bucket and collapsing in a chair. "How's the job going?"

"Okay, I think. No complaints so far," Linda replied, hedging.

"Are you getting along with Gorgeous George?" Maggie quizzed.

Linda giggled. "You sound just like Craig Jensen. He's always calling Jeff things like that."

"The subject invites those comparisons. And who's Craig Jensen?"

Linda described the other lawyer and their encounter with Jeff and Diane the previous night.

"So what's she like?" Maggie asked, interested.

"Actually, she's rather nice, not quite what I expected. She's no Einstein—she won't be curing cancer or pioneering laser surgery—but she'll be a correct, socially acceptable wife who'll wear the right clothes and say the right thing. You can tell she's been groomed to be a wonderful hostess. Together they'll raise beautiful blond children like the kids in a Malibu summer camp."

"That sounds like a sour note," Maggie challenged. "Perhaps she does get under your skin a little."

"Hmmm...maybe a little."

"You think he should be able to tell she's nothing more than a talking ornament."

"I guess that's it."

Maggie made a disgusted noise and pulled off the bandanna that had held her hair back off her face while she was cleaning. "Love is blind, haven't you heard? And if you ask me, he's pretty ornamental himself."

Maggie was not the most generous of souls on the subject of love these days. Divorced for three years, she had recently ended a relationship that for a while had seemed as if it would become permanent. With each disappointment Maggie seemed to get more cautious and cynical. Linda understood the source of her feelings, but she wished her friend would have some good luck with a man that might make her less critical of men.

They emptied Maggie's dishwasher and straightened

up the kitchen while discussing some of their mutual acquaintances from Legal Aid. Maggie snapped her fingers. "That reminds me. Guess who I saw yesterday?"

Linda made several attempts to guess, and Maggie finally said in frustration, "Warren Vanders! And he was very interested in what you were up to."

Linda groaned with real feeling. "I hope you told him I moved to Brazil."

Maggie laughed wickedly. "I told him that you had been asking me about him recently and would probably appreciate a call from him to get back in touch."

Linda's eyes widened with alarm, and she advanced on Maggie. "That had better be a joke."

Maggie grinned and held up her hands in surrender. "It is."

Linda breathed a sigh of relief. Warren Vanders was the single biggest pest in the Western hemisphere, and due to a perverse trick of fate he had decided, about a year before, that he was madly in love with Linda. She had tried everything short of murder to get rid of him. She had finally told him that if he didn't stop calling her, she would report him to the police. He had desisted after that, but he had been difficult to avoid altogether, since his accounting office was in the same building as Legal Aid's. One of the advantages of Linda's job change had been the assurance that she wouldn't unexpectedly run into Warren's hangdog face when she rounded a bend in the corridor.

"His torch was in full blaze," Maggie said. "I actually felt sorry for him."

"You wouldn't feel sorry for him if he were calling you at 3:00 A.M. to make sure you were in bed," Linda said darkly. "When I need a bodyguard, I'll hire one."

Maggie fluffed her short hair with her fingers. "How

about making a shopping trip to Hartford with me next weekend? I need some clothes and I feel the urge to get out of Springfield for a few hours, mecca of culture though it is."

"I can't," Linda said. "I got roped into a benefit basketball game with the pediatric staff at the hospital. I promised I would play."

"Promised who? Oh, I get it. I see the fine hand of Jefferson the third in this," she teased.

"He asked me—what could I say? They need women on the team, and it's for a good cause, though I can't say I'm looking forward to it."

"Well, I am," Maggie said with relish. "I wouldn't miss it for the world. What time does it start, and where? Your cheering section will be in good voice."

"It's at two o'clock in the YMCA downtown. They have a costume party and a bonfire at night. The money from the tickets goes into research and equipment. Why don't you bring Larry?"

Larry was a chemist for a plastics company whom Maggie had met while prosecuting the company in a personal injury case. Linda found him a little dull, but he seemed to be what Maggie needed now. Her husband had been a flamboyant bon vivant who couldn't resist spreading in *joie de vivre* to all of the available women in Massachusetts, and her most recent flame had sky-dived on the weekend for kicks. Larry, on the other hand, did crossword puzzles and played chess.

"I'm not sure that would be Larry's idea of fun," Maggie replied, "though it would be hard to say what would appeal to Larry, other than a vicious double crostic. I'll ask him."

Linda was glad that Maggie would be there. She had the feeling she would need the moral support.

* * *

The day of the game was overcast and raw, with a chill wind, a real precursor of winter. Linda dressed in shorts and a tank top, pulling on loose slacks and a rope-stitch sweater over her playing clothes. She carried her Adidas sneakers and socks in a gym bag, feeling slightly silly, like a suburban housewife who has tennis togs and a hand-strung racket but doesn't know how to play.

Most of the participants were already there, warming up, when Linda arrived and shed her outer clothing. She spotted Jeff doing lay-ups. He was wearing a T-shirt that said, "If you think a tort is an Italian dessert..." on the front, and "...you need a lawyer" on the back.

Susan Daley, one of the paralegals and another female member of the firm's team, came up to Linda, who stood on the sidelines.

"Should we join in or stand here waiting to be asked, like wallflowers at the senior prom?" she asked.

That did seem ridiculous, so Linda answered, "Let's do it."

They practiced passing together in a corner of the floor. "Don't you think we should have had a few practice sessions first?" Linda asked Susan worriedly. "I don't think I'm going to do very well."

Susan smiled. "You mistake the purpose of this little exhibition. They"—she gestured to the rapidly filling stands—"are not here to see us be good, they're here to see us be *entertaining*."

Some of Linda's confidence was restored after she handled the ball for a while. Her tactile memory responded to the feel of the grainy vinyl between her palms, the size and shape of the ball. Even the rubbery smell was familiar, with good associations: camaraderie and hot showers after a tiring but rewarding workout.

They paused for a moment to watch some of the men

dribbling and taking shots. "They're all so good," Linda said.

"Remember where you are," Susan responded. "This is Springfield. Naismith invented the game here, the Basketball Hall of Fame is here. Everybody plays basketball in Springfield."

"Everybody is a fan too," Linda added, commenting on the turnout. She saw Diana, taking a seat in the second row, dressed in designer jeans and a lemon merino sweater. The senior partners were there with their wives, and their children too. Linda had had no idea it was such a big event, and had a suspicion that Jeff had deliberately played it down in order to get her to participate. Well, she was committed now, so she had better make the best of it.

The referees were high-school coaches, and they blew the whistles to clear the floor.

Jeff approached Linda and Susan, handing them both pinnies to tie on over their tops. "We're the shirts, and they're the skins," he said, smiling at Linda. She didn't smile back.

"Hey, relax, it's only a game," he said.

"Tell that to my quaking knees," Linda answered.

Susan wandered off to talk to a friend, and Jeff took Linda's chin in his hand. "You'll be all right," he said, tilting her face up to look at him, and in that moment she knew she would be.

The crowd was settling down. Jeff took Linda's pinny and slipped it over her head, knotting the tie at the back of her waist. Then he patted her fanny lightly like a quarterback giving an "atta boy" to his pass receiver. "Go get 'em," he said softly, and trotted off to center court.

The referee assembled the starting team and explained that they would be playing by high-school rules, with two sixteen-minute halves, divided into two eight-minute quarters each. In the event of a tie score at the end of the game, they would go into a three-minute overtime. There would be a ten-minute break between halves.

He went on to detail some more of the technical information, most of which was familiar to Linda from her playing days. She sat beside Susan on the bench and studied Jeff in the center circle, waiting for the initial jump.

He was charged up, vibrating with eagerness. You could almost see the adrenaline surging through his veins. He was straining like a thoroughbred at the starting gate.

The referee flung the ball into the air, and Jeff and his opponent, an intern named Goldblum, surged upward, like rockets. Jeff tapped the ball to a teammate, and the game began.

It soon became apparent that Jeff was in his element. Too light for the body contact of football, impatient with the slow pace of baseball, he was ideally suited for basketball: tall, slim, and quicksilver-fast. He and Goldblum dominated the game from the start, but Linda's eyes never left Jeff.

The teams were closely matched, and the contest was furious. Both Linda and Susan substituted in the first half, to give the starters a rest. Linda astonished herself by scoring a field goal from just outside the key. Her guard had made the mistake of underestimating her; she saw from his expression when her shot swished through the hoop that he wouldn't repeat the error.

The crowd was having a great time. Noisy and enthusiastic, they screamed and leaped to their feet every time a point was scored. When the buzzer sounded for the end of the second period, the teams left the floor, blending with the spectators. Linda saw Diana standing with a proprietary hand on Jeff's arm, and she turned away from the sight.

"I want an autograph," Maggie said, directly behind her with Larry, "and I'm drawing up a contract when I get home to make me your exclusive agent when the Celtics make their first bid for your services."

Linda laughed, still noticing Jeff and Diana walking past out of the corner of her eye. Maggie saw the object of her gaze and jerked a thumb in Jeff's direction.

"Is there anything he can't do?" she asked, referring to Jeff's performance in the game.

"I don't think he's climbed Mount Everest yet," Linda said.

"Perhaps he's waiting for the spring thaw," Maggie quipped sourly.

"He's got eyes for you," Larry told Linda, and both she and Maggie stared at him. This was such an amazing piece of information, coming from Larry, who normally said very little, that they were stunned into silence.

Larry's skin turned a dull red, but he stuck to his guns. "I was watching him when you made that basket," he continued defensively. "From the expression on his face you would have thought someone had handed him the keys to Fort Knox."

"He already has a duplicate set," Maggie said. "They were given to him at birth, along with the silver spoon."

"Come on, Maggie, give him a break," Linda said. She was getting just a little tired of her friend's constant ribbing.

"Will you listen to this?" Maggie remarked in wonderment. "I do believe that Linda has caught the bug."

Linda was saved from commenting by the start of the second half.

The score had been 54–46 at the end of the first two periods, and it remained close all during the remainder of the game. Jeff seemed to be everywhere, shooting, passing, dribbling downcourt in a rush of motion, his hair a golden blur of light. But he and his teammates were unable to pull far enough ahead to give a safe margin for victory, and the game ended in a tie, putting them into overtime.

Linda was on the floor, having subbed frequently for the first team during the second half. She motioned to Craig, who was managing the roster, to take her out. She didn't want to be in for the final moments. But he shook his head emphatically. Everyone else was too exhausted to be put in.

The clock started again, and Linda unwittingly charged into an opposing player when he abruptly changed direction. She raised her hand to take responsibility for the foul, the other hand on her hip, and then realized that no one was tabulating the violations in this game. She saw Jeff grinning at her unconscious reaction, and shrugged. Old habits were hard to break.

The seconds sped past, and time was running out, when Jeff passed the ball to Linda and she pivoted to make a shot. Goldblum hit her arm as she raised it to release the ball. The ball bounced off the rim, and Linda was awarded two free throws.

Oh, my God, she thought. Tie score with two seconds left, and my foul shots are going to decide the outcome of this game. This was exactly the spot she hadn't wanted to be in, and her throat closed with nervousness.

The players lined up on either side of the foul line as Linda took her place. The referee handed her the ball, and she dribbled it a few times, making sure she was well behind the foul shooting line.

She looked up at the rim of the basket, which seemed about twenty light years away. Then she saw Jeff standing under it, his eyes intent on her. Wordless communication flowed between them. You can do it, his look seemed to say, I know you can.

Linda took a deep breath, forcing herself to concentrate. The hushed, waiting crowd faded, and the years fell away. She was seventeen again, playing the championship game against St. Cecilia's in Englewood, New Jersey. She had done it then, and she could do it now. Jeff was right.

She raised the ball to her eye level, placing her fingertips on the side seams, anchoring her feet. Then she thrust it up and out, watching as it sailed cleanly through the net.

The crowd stirred but did not erupt. She had another shot. The ball was returned to her, and she bounced it a few times, trying to reach again that level of readiness. When she released it this time, the watchers were already shouting before it dropped in, and they sounded like a single overwhelming voice, a wall of noise. Jeff grabbed the ball off the backboard and held it while the two seconds passed. The game was over, and the shirts had won.

Jeff threw the ball down and rushed to Linda, sweeping her up in his arms and lifting her as if she were weightless. They were both overheated, excited, on a natural high. At another time the impact of their bodies touching might not have been so strong, but the heady moment of success made them vulnerable.

The cords in Jeff's arms stood out like bands, enfolding her in a circle of steel. Her face was pressed against his chest, and she could feel the pumping of his heart under her ear. Unthinking, she put her arms around his neck, and she felt his answering response, a tightening of his muscles, a small sigh that she heard despite the clamor around them. When she raised her head to look into his eyes, she saw in them a reflection of her own

desire. The incident that day at his house had not been
a fluke. Their whole relationship changed in that fraction
of a second when their gazes met, and they knew there
was no turning back.

Jeff let Linda's feet touch the ground, and her body
slid along his as she got her balance. His eyes closed,
and his hands dropped from her waist, clenching into
fists. He feels it as much as I do, Linda thought, and
she was frightened. What was going to happen? She had
never known this kind of need, even with Jim, and it
made her feel powerless, out of control. In the grip of
it, she might do anything.

The crowd moved around them, and she fled, leaving
Jeff standing, shell-shocked, in the middle of the gym.

The YMCA had only one locker room, and the men
waited while the women took showers. Linda hurried
through hers, wishing that she had not told Craig that
she would attend the bonfire and the party. She left with
her hair still wet, and went home to change.

The day had grown colder as the afternoon waned,
and Linda rooted through her wardrobe, looking for
something that would be warm and comfortable. She
settled on plaid wool slacks and a thick, hand-knit fish-
erman's sweater. She packed the costume she and Maggie had created in an overnight bag and waited for Craig
to pick her up.

He was going as the Hunchback of Notre Dame, and
she would be Esmeralda. Craig had gotten a grotesque
mask, and planned on stuffing a pillow inside his shirt
for the hump. The rest of his costume consisted of ragged
clothing of which, he assured Linda, there was no short-
age in his closet.

Linda had agreed to his suggestion because her costume was easy. A gypsy outfit was assembled from odds

and ends that she already had. An embroidered peasant blouse coupled with a full, flowered skirt formed the base, and Linda added lots of jewelry, dangling earrings, a colorful scarf, and exaggerated makeup. As she listened for the sound of Craig's car in her driveway, she hoped she wasn't encouraging him too much by going with him, but she just couldn't face another stag appearance when Diana would be with Jeff. She felt uncomfortably like she was using the easygoing, likable Craig, and her conscience was bothering her.

The bonfire was set on the high-school athletic field, and there were a number of cars in the lot when Linda and Craig arrived in his M.G. Several charcoal barbecues had been placed on the cement patio behind the auditorium, and the smell of roasting hot dogs and hamburgers filled the air. Linda realized that she was very hungry. The game and the cold weather had helped her to work up an appetite. She and Craig went over to get something to eat, and Linda watched the men piling up wood and kindling in the October dusk. A cheer went up from the group when they set the pyre alight.

She was munching her hot dog when she saw Jeff and Diana walking along the outskirts of the milling crowd. Jeff wore beige corduroy chinos with a tattersall flannel shirt and a dark green trail vest. Diana still wore her jeans from the afternoon but had added a red anorak to combat the cold. They both had on suede desert boots, and looked ready to backpack through the Berkshires. They were young, healthy, and vibrant. Linda glanced down at the rest of her hot dog in her hand and threw it in the trash.

The fire soon escalated to a roaring blaze, and old hands at this annual event had brought along army blankets and Hudson's Bay comforters to spread on the ground around it. Craig took a canvas cover from the trunk of his little car, and he and Linda settled in next to Dr. Goldblum and his pretty wife, who had a beautiful, ringing voice, and led the enthusiastic following in familiar songs. Linda felt as if she were with the Girl Scouts on a camp-out, and her mind drifted to childhood memories of happy times spent in the North Jersey woods with Laurie and Karen and all her old friends, some of whom she hadn't seen in years. Dreamy, distant, she didn't object when Craig slipped his arm about her shoulders and pulled her close.

She stared into the flames until she became aware that someone was staring at her. She looked up and met Jeff's eyes across the distance. He was sitting cross-legged on the ground, reminding her of when she found him in his kitchen, fixing his toaster. His arms were wrapped around his knees, and his face was serious, thoughtful. Diana was nowhere to be seen.

Linda sat up, disengaging herself from Craig's grasp, and thrust her hands forward to the fire. After a moment she stood restlessly and told Craig she was going to get some coffee. He offered to get it for her, but she told him she wanted to walk around a bit. He shrugged and stretched out full length on the tarpaulin, propping his chin in his hands.

Linda wandered away from the activity, stopping at a table manned by the pediatric wives for a styrofoam cup of coffee. The sound of the singing became muffled and choirlike as she rounded the empty bleachers and sat on the bottom step, sipping her coffee. The distant firelight cast a glow in the night sky and danced along the metal facings of the folding supports. She leaned back on her elbows and stared at the winter stars.

A twig snapping behind her made her jump. "Boo," Jeff said. "You're lucky I'm not the Springfield strangler, come to put your neck in a knot. What are you doing out here all by yourself?"

"Thinking," she responded, wondering if he had come after her.

"Well, that's all right, then. Think away."

"Some people might say I do too much thinking," she said, remembering Jim.

"Some people might be wrong. The nicest thing about you is that you're smart."

Linda didn't know how to respond to this compliment, and chose a safe subject instead. "How's Nate?"

"Nate is in love," Jeff answered solemnly. "He's having a mad fling with the French poodle down the street. He is enchanted with her delicacy and fine grooming, and she is overwhelmed by his rakish charm. I feel like an extra on the set of *Lady and the Tramp*."

Linda laughed with him, but there was an edge to it. She had not forgotten that moment at the end of the game that afternoon, and she wagered that he hadn't either. It hung between them, unspoken, flavoring their exchange.

"What time does the party get underway?" she asked.

"Whenever they finish decorating and setting out the goodies, I guess. Diana's in there right now, hanging up pumpkins or whatever. They do a nice job. Last year you could hardly recognize the creaking old auditorium under all the goblin decor."

The mention of Diana's name reminded Linda that she had better get back to Craig and end this dangerous conversation. She knew that she was headed for trouble if she stayed.

"I don't think I congratulated you on your clutch performance today," Jeff said huskily, as if he could read her mind and was seeking a topic to hold her.

Yes, you did, Linda thought, and words weren't necessary.

"I told you that you could handle it," he said. "I'm beginning to think that you can handle anything."

Except you, Jefferson T. Langford, except you. She squeezed her coffee cup into a flattened cylinder and vaulted to her feet.

"Thanks, Jeff. It's nice of you to say so. I think I'd better see where Craig is. See you later."

Craig was looking for her when she got back. "Where did you disappear to?" he asked curiously.

"I went for a walk, as I told you," Linda answered, not wanting to get into a discussion of her whereabouts for the last fifteen minutes, in case Jeff's absence had been noticed also.

"I think we'd better saddle up," Craig said. "They're going to drown this thing"—he indicated the fire—"and go inside shortly."

"I don't know about this"—Linda half-laughed—"bonfires and costume parties, it all seems a bit juvenile, don't you think?"

"That may be," Craig responded, "but I'll tell you one thing, after what I went through to get this job, if Mr. Pinney thought it was a good idea that I spit into the wind upon arising every morning, you'd catch me out there at 7:00 A.M., letting it fly. The powers that be are sponsoring this shindig, and they like to see lots of smiling faces enjoying their sponsorship. They're going to see mine."

Linda nodded. Politics. It was the same everywhere.

They packed up and joined the others moving through the large double doors to the auditorium.

* * *

Linda traced her mouth again with dark lipstick and examined the effect in the spotted mirror over the locker-room sink. She looked exotic, slightly slumberous, and sexy—just what she wanted for Esmeralda, the wanton gypsy girl who had captured the heart of the pitiful hunchback. She adjusted the elasticized, gathered top of the blouse a little lower on her shoulders and tossed her head to make her earrings bounce. Good.

"I think your hair could use a little work," Susan Daley said from across the room, where she was putting the finishing touches on the shepherd's staff of her Little Bo Peep costume.

"What do you mean?"

"It should look a little wilder, like Sophia Loren playing Aldonza in *Man of La Mancha*."

Susan came over to her and took the comb out of her hand. "Let me tease it a little."

She back-combed Linda's dark hair and then smoothed it over, so that it stood out like a nimbus around her head.

"Thanks a lot. I look like I should be hanging out on Seventh Avenue in a plastic jumpsuit."

"Exactly. Esmeralda was not a lady of spotless virtue."

Linda fastened the buttons on the back of Susan's bib and said, "Why didn't they have the game here this afternoon too, since we were going to be here tonight?"

Susan stretched her neck to test the tightness of the collar. "The kids were having a game here this afternoon. Pinney has a lot of influence with the Board of Education, but not enough to get them to cancel a scheduled athletic event so his employees could party. He's on the managing board for the YMCA, and that's how we wound up there."

They studied each other, and were satisfied. "Let's

go," Susan said. "I don't know how long this papier mache staff is going to hold up, and I want to get some use out of it before it disintegrates."

Craig was a convincing hunchback. He had perfected a lurching, shambling walk that actually made him look deformed, and the mask was a horror.

"Quasimodo!" Linda exclaimed, when she saw him. "How are things in the bell tower?"

"Hot," he grumbled, his voice muffled by the mask. "This rubber face is suffocating me."

"Take it off," Susan said. "Nobody will notice the difference."

"You're hilarious," Craig said to her. "I suppose you think you look fetching in that rig?"

"My sheep like it," Susan said airily, and went off in search of her date.

Linda and Craig bent low under the hanging crepe-paper streamers of orange and black and entered a fun-house world of skeletons suspended from the ceiling and flickering jack o' lanterns set along the upper balconies. Linda was fascinated by the varied, imaginative costumes she saw on display around the hall. Craig led her to the refreshment table, where they each took a cup of punch.

"What happens now?" Linda asked.

"Oh, you'll see. They have contests and games, bobbing for apples, the usual stuff. And I think they've got a rock band this year—Rolf's nephew, or somebody like that. The party will warm up once the music starts."

It did. By nine o'clock the gym was full, and the deafening music precluded any attempt at conversation, so everybody danced. The vibrations from the electric instruments thrummed in the floor and bounced off the walls. Linda had had enough after about half an hour, and begged off to go to the ladies room to try to restore her hearing.

She had just begun to search for an emery board in her purse to repair a hangnail when the door opened and Diana Northrup came in. She was a vision of loveliness, in a floor-length gown and jeweled tiara. She smiled when she saw Linda.

"Why, hello. Who are you tonight?"

"Esmeralda from *The Hunchback of Notre Dame.*"

Diana nodded appreciatively. "Very clever. Jeff and I are doing 'The Frog Prince.' He's the prince and I'm the princess."

You certainly are, Linda thought. Diana's dress was pale lavender, with a fitted bodice and a wide skirt over-laid with net. It had a square neck with spaghetti straps, and a gleaming amethyst necklace picked up and re-flected the color of the material. Her hair was piled high on her head, caught in a topknot of curls by the sparkling ornament. If you think Jeff is even going to look at you with this one around, Linda said to herself, there's a bridge in Brooklyn that you ought to buy.

"You look the part," Linda said, truthfully enough.

She made short work of filing her nail and left, with a final self-conscious smile at Diana.

When she went back into the auditorium the first person she saw was Jeff. He was wearing frog flippers on his hands and feet, and a frog mask was pushed back up on his head. A green body suit was enhanced by a short cape hanging from his shoulders, and a small gold crown was set in his hair. The picture was clear: half frog, half prince. Even in the ridiculous costume, he was attractive.

Linda eventually found Craig in the midst of a limbo contest. The field had been narrowed to four, and the bar was so low that Linda could not imagine a human body flexible enough to fit under it. She watched the dancers' contortions for a while, applauding the feats of agility, and booing when one of the contestants bumped the pole. The winner was a resident at the hospital, a skinny, sandy-haired gymnast who held aloft his prize, a statuette engraved "World's Best Dancer."

The band took a break, for which Linda was grateful, and she and Craig sat on a couple of the folding chairs placed along the sides of the dance floor. Craig mopped his brow with a handkerchief and said, "Could you get me something to drink, please? I'd do it, but I'm not sure I can walk after that."

Linda went to the back of the hall, and was served by a familiar-looking woman in her forties with wavy salt-and-pepper hair. She smiled at Linda and said, "You're Ms. Redfield, aren't you?"

"Yes."

"I'm Phyllis Beresford, Roger's wife."

Roger Beresford was one of the bigwigs at the firm. He had a lot of influence locally; his uncle had been a councilman and his grandfather a lieutenant governor of the state. He wasn't a full partner, but he was everything else. Though Linda had not yet worked with him, she had a nodding acquaintance with him.

"How do you do, Mrs. Beresford?"

"Oh, Phyllis, please. We don't stand on ceremony here. I hope young Jensen is showing you around, making you feel at home. I saw you coming in with him. Actually, I was surprised. My husband told me Jeff Langford's son was responsible for your hiring, and I thought he might be escorting you."

"He did suggest me for the position, yes, but we don't see each other socially. He's here with Diana Northrup."

"I see," said Mrs. Beresford, in a tone that suggested she didn't see at all.

"Thanks for the drink," Linda said, and walked away. She was in no mood to be grilled by a society type who only wanted grist for her gossip mill. Things must be pretty dull up in Northampton if Mrs. Beresford had to resort to interrogating her husband's coworkers for topics of interest.

Craig downed his drink in one gulp and pulled Linda onto the floor when the band blared into action again. She kept up with him for two or three dances, and then, turning to walk back to her chair, almost barged into Jeff.

"Hi," he said. "Have a fin." He handed her one of his flippers, which was actually a glove with extended fingers, and scratched his nose.

"There he is," Craig said, joining them and looking Jeff over from head to foot.

Jeff laughed. "If I look half as outrageous as I feel, I'm in a lot of trouble."

Linda looked around for Diana but didn't see her.

"The worst thing about this costume is that it itches," Jeff went on. "I'm trying to keep in character, and I can't remember if frogs scratch."

"They croak," Craig remarked dryly. "Croaking is what they're into."

"I'll be croaking too, if this gala lasts much longer. Frog suits are definitely not on my list of favorite things," Jeff grunted.

Craig put an arm around Linda's shoulders, and Jeff's face clouded. Linda did not want to shrug Craig's arm off, but she wished he hadn't put it there.

"How's this fellow been treating you?" Jeff asked her, looking at her intently, his voice low.

"Don't worry about it, Jeff," Craig answered for her. "If she has any complaints, she'll let you know, and your father can put in the word to fire me."

He chuckled, and then saw that Linda and Jeff were not laughing. "Hey, you two, that was a joke," he added.

"I don't think Linda found it very amusing," Jeff said quietly.

Craig looked from one to the other, and then took his arm away from Linda. "I get the feeling I've missed something. Since I seem to be somewhat *de trop* right now, I'll push off." Looking back over his shoulder at Linda, he blended into the crowd.

"It still bothers you, doesn't it?" Jeff asked her. "What you perceive as my elevated status?"

She wasn't going to get into that discussion again. "Drop it, Jeff. It was just a thoughtless remark. Craig didn't mean anything by it."

They were standing on the floor, with the dancers weaving about them. "Let's get out of here," Jeff said, taking Linda's hand.

She could hardly get into a tug of war with him on the dance floor, so she allowed herself to be dragged along. He took her into the empty cooridor, lined with steel lockers and glass trophy cases.

They looked at each other, and Linda cast about for something innocuous to say.

"I like that costume," she offered brightly. "I've always loved that story. Imagine, starting out with a frog and winding up with a prince. My problem is, I keep starting out with princes and winding up with frogs."

"Perhaps you're not performing the transformation properly," Jeff said. "It's done with a kiss. Allow me to demonstrate."

Before she could react, he had drawn her to him and covered her mouth with his. At first the pressure was light, then more intense, until she was clutching him, trembling, aware of nothing but the lips that caressed hers, the arms that held her so tightly. His mouth moved to her neck, her earlobes, the hollow at the base of her throat. Her whole world was reduced to the burning sensation of his lips on her skin. He pushed aside the shoulders of her blouse and kissed the tops of her breasts, his hands seeking the soft flesh that swelled the cloth beneath.

Linda heard a sound from the hall, and sensibility returned like a dash of cold water in the face. She pulled away from Jeff, her eyes wide, her skin flooding scarlet at the awareness of what they had done.

She stared at Jeff in the artificial light of the corridor. His lips and teeth were stained with her lipstick, giving him the look of a postprandial vampire. She pulled a tissue from the pocket of her skirt and wiped off the garish smears. He stood still under her ministering hand, watching her.

"Jeff, we must put this out of our minds," Linda said in an unsteady voice. "It was a mistake. Let's not mention it again."

He was so motionless, he appeared to be holding his breath. Then he bent from the waist in a courtly bow. "I shall do my best to obey you, madam."

When Linda went to the rest room to collect her wits, she saw in the mirror that her throat and bosom were brushed with red. The lipstick had been carried there by Jeff's mouth. She felt uncomfortable, as if she had been marked in some way, stamped with the imprint of his possession.

She scrubbed the stains off industriously before she left.

Chapter Five

AFTER LUNCH ONE lovely afternoon, the eighth week of her tenure with Langford's firm, Linda was trying to make some sense out of an eighteenth-century case when Jeff knocked on her door.

He was wearing a navy blazer with khaki slacks and cordovan loafers, a pale blue shirt and dark knit tie completing the picture. He looked the image of what he was, a young man whose faith in himself was so inbred that he took it for granted. Linda envied him that birthright, that unshakable conviction that he could take on the world and win.

He pulled back his cuff to examine his watch. "I'm going downtown. Got anything at the jail?"

He was offering to run an errand for her. His open generosity was an aspect of his personality that continually confused Linda. She was almost ashamed of herself for finding it suspect. Also, Jeff was completely accepting of her role in the Puritan project. He considered her ideas, implemented her suggestions, weighed her opinions—in short, treated her as an equal partner. Even though that was exactly what he should have done, Linda kept waiting for the facade to crack. It was gradually dawning on her that perhaps he wasn't just pretending to be a kind, decent human being, but actually was one.

She glanced at the pile of folders that she'd received from the other attorneys when she'd started at the firm. They had each given her a few cases in addition to the one she was working on with Jeff. Linda pulled a file from the bottom and looked at her notes, stapled to the inside front cover. "There's a Stanley Wellington being held for assault. I really should talk to him today."

Jeff grinned, and she was momentarily dazzled by the force of that smile. "You inherited old Stanley?" he said. "Oh, you're in for a treat. Well, if you want to come along, my chariot awaits. I've got to stop at police headquarters on the way back."

Linda put aside her colonial puzzle and picked up her purse along with Wellington's file. She followed Jeff out to the reception area, waiting while he told Mary where they were going.

"Stanley is something of a tradition around here," Jeff explained as they got into the elevator. "He comes from a staid old family, which is why he's our client, but he's been disowned for many years. He lives at a rooming house downtown and gets plastered and into a fight every six weeks or so. There is a trust fund, but his family is at the point where they just refuse to bail him out anymore. Each time he gets picked up, his bond gets higher and he cools his heels in the lockup a little longer. He'll doubtless tell you which of his reprobate friends is currently able to put up the money." Jeff turned up his collar against the autumn wind. "It would be a pathetic story except that Stanley is deliriously happy and wouldn't have it any other way. The lawyers at the firm pass him around like a head cold. I guess you were dealt him due to your position as low man...uh, person...on the totem pole."

Linda couldn't wait to see this character. Jeff spoke further while fishing in his pocket for car keys. "As you've probably noticed, the firm handles very few criminal cases, usually only those involving the families or friends of business clients. I've got one today too—the son of a friend of my father's, picked up with an assortment of drugs sufficient to open a pharmacy. The kid's a screwball. He stands to inherit five million dollars at the age of twenty-one, and at nineteen is traveling interstate with three kilos of hash, four ounces of coke, and enough angel dust to turn an entire convent of nuns into crazed green berets." He shook his head. "Worse, he's been arrested before. He's also a user. It's a sad case."

As they got in the car, Jeff pushed a button to roll the windows down, and the brisk autumn breeze stirred Linda's hair.

"They just brought him in and are holding him in the county tank until I see him. They'll take him up to Walpole, and then through the long gray tunnel to oblivion." He glanced at Linda, and the expressive jade eyes were filled with such pain that she almost touched him in her urge to comfort. Her fingers flexed, then relaxed. He looked back at the road.

"I remember him as a kid when I was in school. He used to build model planes."

Linda was silent. What could she say? They both knew that federal drug laws were sure to put the boy away for a long time, especially since he was a repeater. The look in Jeff's eyes remained in her mind. This wasn't just a job to him. He recalled a little boy he'd liked, and was

now unable to help the adult. Linda stared out the passenger window, and her expression grew thoughtful.

The jail was an old stone structure that always smelled
damp. Linda identified herself to the desk sergeant and
was ushered into the visiting room, with its frosted glass
door and ancient scarred wooden table. Jeff wandered
over to the main desk and talked to the officer on duty.

After a few minutes, the door opened and a guard
looked in. He took in Linda in her blue blouse and char-
coal-gray skirt, sitting demurely at the table. He smiled.

"You the lawyer?"

Linda nodded.

His smile became wider, and he said over his shoulder, "There you go, Stanley, your troubles are over. Your
lawyer's here to save you." He dissolved into laughter
as the prisoner shuffled in and he took up his station
outside the door.

Stanley Wellington was a man of indeterminate middle age. He wore a brown tweed jacket, which had obviously been of fine quality but was now stained and
abused. He had a three-days' growth of grayish stubble
on his face below shrewd watery eyes. A Red Sox baseball cap was jammed backwards on his head, and a "Split
Wood, not Atoms" button was pinned to his lapel. He
surveyed Linda suspiciously.

"Where's Joe?" he said.

"Joe?"

"Joe Axelrod, my lawyer. Who are you?"

"Mr. Wellington, you are represented by the firm of
Rolf, Langford and Pinney. As such, any lawyer from
the firm can handle your case. It's been given to me."

Wellington nodded. "So they stuck the rookie with
me, huh?"

Linda said nothing.

"Well, no matter. Look, miss, can you get this feller

on the phone? Here's his name and number—he'll go the bail. Can you do that?"

"I think I'm capable of handling it, Mr. Wellington," Linda said dryly, taking the proffered scrap of paper.

Wellington started to go. "Don't you think we should discuss your case?" she called after him.

"Oh, no, it's just the usual. Get me out, is all I ask." He moved toward the door again, and then turned back to whisper conspiratorily, "Good for you. I think it's great, you girls getting to be doctors and lawyers and all that. I'm an advocate of Women's Lib, you know." He winked and shambled out. Linda spotted a paperback copy of James Joyce's *Dubliners* peeking from his back pocket.

Linda was still chuckling to herself when she joined Jeff at the main desk.

"So what did you think of Stanley?" he asked with a grin.

"I'm going to send him in to *Reader's Digest* as the 'Most Unforgettable Character I've Met.'"

"He's something, all right," Jeff agreed. "The first time he met me, he did my astrological charts and told me I had a previous incarnation as a Greek slave doctor in ancient Rome."

Linda started to laugh. "You're making that up."

He raised his hand like a witness taking the oath, his face a mask of innocence. "I swear to God. He said I was an herbalist named Anaxamander who was personal physician to the nephew of the emperor Tiberius."

"Okay, I'll believe you."

He shrugged. "You ask Stanley next time you see him. And I'm sure you'll be seeing him again."

"Thanks a lot."

They went round the corner to the police department, Linda matching her stride to Jeff's long one. "Do you want to come in with me?" Jeff said. "I'll introduce you to my friend Claude Delancey. He's chief of detectives."

Linda thought this was an unlikely friend for Jeff to have, and was interested to meet him. "Okay."

They went through the wide, leaded double doors into the station, where Jeff was told that his client was being fingerprinted. They could see him in the holding area.

Linda followed Jeff down a gray-painted hall to an open room with several booking desks. A plainclothesman sat at one of them taking a statement from a young man.

The boy was dressed in faded jeans, a denim jacket, and sturdy laced work boots. His dark blond hair fell in loose waves from a ragged center part, and his lower face was obscured by a full brown beard. A heavy silver chain was looped from his belt to his back pocket.

He looked up at Jeff without a sign of recognition. "Hello, Bobby," Jeff said.

The boy's eyes moved from Jeff to the policeman to Linda. Then he was up in a blur of motion. Before anyone could stop him, he had snatched a letter opener from the desk and grabbed Linda, his arm about her throat. With his other hand he held the point of the metal piece under Linda's chin.

"Jeff, you tell these pigs to turn me loose or I'm gonna stick your girlfriend here. This shiv is pretty dull, but if I jab it hard enough it ought to do some damage. I don't think you want to find out." While Jeff stood silent, stunned, Bobby pulled up on Linda's neck so that her air supply was restricted. She moaned, and Jeff made a move toward her. "She's dead meat if you try anything, Jeff," the boy warned, and Jeff stepped back. His eyes never left Linda's face.

Linda had never been so terrified in her life. Fear was a coppery taste in her mouth, and for the first time in a long time she prayed. The prayers from her childhood ran through her horrified mind like a chant.

The man holding her smelled terribly. He was flushed and sweating, and Linda could almost feel his heart racing. Even in her shock she realized that he must be insane to try something like this in the middle of a police station surrounded by cops. All the onlookers had frozen in place like participants in a tableau.

Jeff found his voice. "Bobby, let her go. I promise I'll get you the best deal possible. You're higher than a kite, man, you don't know what you're doing. You'll never get away with this. If you hurt the girl, you're finished, and even if you don't and try to get away, you'll be nailed before you take a step. Bobby, please. I can't help you if you do this. Think, man, think."

Linda imagined her captor's reason trying to overcome his drug-induced panic. Slowly his iron grip relaxed. Jeff saw it and said, "Drop the cutter, Bob." She was shoved forward roughly as she heard the metal object hit the floor.

Without thinking, purely instinctively, she ran straight into Jeff's arms. He caught her and held her against his chest, caressing her hair, soothing her. "It's all right now, you're safe. It's all over," his voice murmured softly in her ear. She was vaguely aware of the noise around her as Bobby was seized and dragged away.

Jeff's slim appearance was deceptive, Linda discovered as she clung to him, relief singing through her veins. He was muscular and lean, hard; the flesh beneath her tensed hands was spare but firm. She gradually realized that she was clutching him as if she were the delicate heroine of a Victorian melodrama. She was not about to have the vapors in front of a room full of staring people. She gently disengaged herself and stepped back, pushing her disordered hair away from her face. "I'm sorry," she said. "That was very childish of me."

Jeff stood looking down at her, a frown creasing his brow. "Why are you apologizing? We were both scared witless. There's no reason to be sorry."

Linda didn't know what to say to that. She clasped her hands in front of her to stop their shaking. Jeff took her arm. "Why don't you go into Claude's office and sit down for a bit? I'll get you a glass of water."

Linda allowed him to usher her into the empty office, where she was deposited on a leather couch. As Jeff went out, he met a large red-haired man on his way into the room. Linda could hear their conversation through the door.

"Claude, what the hell kind of an outfit are you running here?" Jeff's quiet voice was furious. She had never heard him use that tone before.

"Why wasn't that man cuffed?" Jeff went on. "Anyone with a brain could see he was all hopped up on something. I want him to receive medical attention immediately, and I want a psychiatric work-up done on him before the preliminary hearing, do you understand?"

She could not hear Delancey's response as they walked away, but she saw him clap Jeff on the shoulder reassuringly. Jeff was shaking his head, not mollified. Linda's eyes closed, and she let her head drop to the back of the couch.

A few minutes later Jeff came back with a styrofoam coffee cup filled with water, and a pill. "It's a tranquilizer," he said. "The nurse downstairs gave it to me."

Linda took a sip of the water but declined the pill. "No, thanks. If I start popping these now, I'll be a trembling wreck by the time I'm forty."

"That's the spirit," he said, and dropped it into the wastebasket. He sat beside her and stretched his long legs out in front of him, contemplating his shoes, dead-pan. "So, uh, what's new?"

They looked at each other and broke into laughter. Linda couldn't stop, wiping her eyes and putting her hand to her throat. "I think I'm hysterical," she finally gasped.

"With perfect justification," Jeff answered. He jammed his hands into his pockets and crossed his legs at the ankle. "Well, if I can't interest you in a pill, how about booze? I can at least take you for a drink. It's four-thirty—the day's shot anyway. I feel I should do something. You got involved in this mess because you came here with me."

Linda hesitated. She was vaguely uncomfortable about accompanying him. It was too much like a date. But the urge to be with him overrode her objections. "All right."

She was filled with a sense of anticipation as they left the station. She didn't ask where they were going, but of course his finely tuned manners would not allow him to select a place alone. "Where would you like to go?"

Linda sat back comfortably against the cushioned leather upholstery. "You choose—I'm too spent to think. Surprise me."

He smiled slightly. "One surprise, coming up."

Linda let the smooth motion of the car soothe her. She was dimly aware of Jeff's negotiating the city streets and then that they were on the outskirts of town. As the car glided onto the highway, Jeff glanced over to say something. She met his eyes, started to speak too, and thought better of it.

"Just rest," he agreed, nodding. "You've had a busy day."

They were driving on a two-lane blacktop, between rows of dense trees that provided a riot of color in the autumn landscape. Leaves were thick as a carpet along the roadside, rust and brown and a coppery gold the shade of Jeff's hair. Linda was jolted into full wakefulness as he turned into a country lane and hit a rut.

"Sorry," he said. "The trip is a bit rocky, but it will be worth it. At least, I hope you'll think so."

They pulled up, a few minutes later, to a restored colonial from the late 1700's, with stone facing and a circular gravel carriage path curving in front of it. Jeff parked in a paved lot off to the side, and they walked across the immaculately kept grounds to the wide covered porch. Inside, a young lady in a period outfit complete with mob cap and frilled apron greeted them.

The interior took Linda's breath away. The original woodwork and wide pineboard planking gleamed with a rich finish in the entry hall, where a huge fireplace the width of one whole wall consumed what looked like a small tree. Antique furnishings were used very effectively to add to the gracious atmosphere. A cherry rolltop desk held the guest ledger, and a preserved spinning wheel stood next to a little milking stool. Hooked and braided rugs adorned the polished floors. Linda stood rooted, charmed into silence. Jeff cast her a sidelong glance, looking satisfied at her reaction.

The girl led them to the main dining room, where another, smaller, fireplace cast a cheerful glow. The room was filled with intimate round tables covered with crisp white cloths; embroidered red napkins, as vivid as blood against the snowy linen, were folded at each place. A glass hurricane lamp stood on every table, along with a tiny crystal vase of cut flowers. When they were seated, Linda looked across to Jeff.

"It's perfectly lovely," she said. "How did you know about this place?"

"Actually, it belonged to one of my woodpile ancestors," he replied casually. "He built it for the bride he brought over from England. It does a small but regular business. Not too many people know about it."

"That way only the right people will patronize it, right?"

He held up his hand as if to declare a truce. "No speeches tonight, okay?"

Linda relented. "Okay."

A steward appeared, and Jeff ordered a bottle of white wine. Linda rarely drank and so did not recognize the name, but she probably wouldn't have anyway. Doubtless it was something the upper crust kept in cool dark cellars to be uncorked at the appropriate time. The man left, and Jeff handed Linda a menu.

"Let's have dinner," he said. "I haven't eaten since eleven thirty this morning, and if I drink that wine on an empty stomach, I'll be reeling around and embarrass you."

Linda hesitated. He guessed the source of her discomfort and said quietly, "No strings."

That made her feel foolish, so she quickly glanced down at the list of dishes and selected a seafood cocktail and stuffed flounder. Jeff ordered pâté and lobster tails. Even though she knew the expense was nothing to him, she marveled at the ease with which he spent money.

At seven-thirty, two hostesses opened the sliding double doors at one end of the room, to reveal a band assembled on a raised platform in the alcove beyond and a circular dance floor. The soft music filled the air, and couples drifted dreamily to the melodies, while the lamplight reflected upon them through windows.

Linda nervously picked at her food when it arrived. When Jeff had asked her to join him for a drink, she hadn't counted on this romantic atmosphere or the leisurely pace of a full dinner. They talked little during the meal; Jeff seemed reserved also. When the dishes were cleared and they had refused dessert, he extracted a cigarette from an ivory case in his breast pocket and lit it with a gold lighter.

"I didn't know you smoked," Linda said.

"I don't usually," he replied. "Only when I'm tense or..." He broke off, realizing what he had admitted. He actually blushed, and Linda was captivated. He wasn't as sure of himself as he seemed. He recovered quickly and grinned. "But I do penance for it by jogging every day."

He ordered coffee and brandy, and they sat listening to the band. Jeff hummed along with the selections. Finally he crushed his cigarette in the ashtray and stood by her chair, extending his hand. "Will you dance with me, or do I have to ask the waitress?"

Knowing it was a mistake but unable to stop herself, Linda got up and followed him to the dance floor. Once there, he pulled her into his arms with practiced ease. She remembered the intoxication of him from that afternoon when he had held her. She tried not to cling, but the music and the wine lulled her, until she was dancing with her head on his shoulder and her arms about his neck. This is madness, this is madness, said a voice in her mind. But she pushed it aside and listened to her body, which wanted to blend with this man completely. One of his hands was flat against her back, and it moved caressingly up her spine to touch the hair at the nape of her neck. She could feel his body heat rising, and he seemed to vibrate with tensile strength. Her eyes closed as she melted into him, feeling the answering tightening of his arms. God help me, she thought, don't let him see how I feel.

Abruptly, the music stopped. Linda didn't know whether to cry or murmur a prayer of thanksgiving. The band drifted off to take a break, as Jeff released her, with obvious reluctance. They stood in the middle of the floor, and Linda avoided his eyes. She turned swiftly and went back to the table. After a moment, he followed, more slowly.

They drank their coffee in a strained silence. Linda noticed that he gulped down his brandy, while she left hers untouched. She had originally planned to offer to pay for her share, but Jeff just signed the check, and she felt ridiculous for the thought. She picked up her purse and murmured that she was going to the powder room.

Her eyes looked unnaturally bright in the gilt-edged mirror, though her face was pale. Her hands were ice cold. I have to get this relationship back on a professional level, she thought. He must never suspect how much he disturbed her, or working with him would be impossible. But even as these thoughts crossed her mind, Linda felt the imprint of his body against hers. She yanked a comb through her hair and applied lipstick, which made her features look ghostly. Hastily wiping it off again, she pinched her cheeks. That was better.

Jeff was waiting for her in the lobby with her blazer over his arm. He helped her into it silently, and they went outside. Linda shivered violently, whether from emotional reaction or contact with the chill night air she could not say. But Jeff noticed it, as he seemed to notice everything, and he removed his suit jacket, draping it over her shoulders. When she protested he said curtly, "Take it. Don't be silly." Something in the tone of his voice brooked no argument, so she shrugged into its warmth gratefully.

The walk to the car was silent and so was the drive home. Jeff put a tape of Van Cliburn playing Tchaikovsky's First on the tape deck, eliminating the necessity of talking, though he did ask her if she wanted to go to her car or straight home. Linda thought for a moment. Her car was locked and insured, and she was tired. She could take a cab in the morning, so she told Jeff to take her home.

When they arrived at her house, Jeff moved to get out and walk her to the door, but she put a restraining hand on his arm. He watched her as she slipped out of his coat and laid it on the back of the seat. As she reached for the door handle he said, "Linda." She turned back and held a finger to his lips. He kissed it gently, his mouth soft and warm on her skin. Stunned, she stared at him. He released her hand and said quietly, "All right, counselor, we won't talk about it. Good night."

She walked up the porch steps, unlocking the door mechanically. He waited until she was safely inside before driving away. Linda closed the door and sagged against it, gingerly caressing the place his lips had touched.

A few days later Jeff found the clue to the framework of the case they were trying to build for Puritan. It was the end of the afternoon, and Linda was vaguely aware that everyone else in the office was packing up and leaving. The hubbub of typewriter keys and the opening and closing of filing cabinets ceased, replaced by "Good-byes" and "see you tomorrows." But Linda worked on, flipping through dozens of old cases in the reporters, scanning the head notes for ideas. It was 5:45 when Jeff appeared in her doorway. Linda looked up, surprised. She thought he had gone home with the others.

"Eureka," he said quietly. "I've found it."

Despite his mild tone, she could see that he was alive with excitement. His glasses were shoved up in his thick hair like a visor, his tie was off, and the sleeves of his shirt were rolled up to the elbows. In his hands he brandished an old, worn volume, *King's Bench, 1812*.

"Eighteen-twelve? Forget it, that thing's been over-ruled a million times," Linda told him.

Jeff shook his head. "It has not. I had the clerk Shepardize it twice and I did it once myself. And," he added, pausing dramatically, "it was used as authority in Pennsylvania in 1973. Listen to this." He leaned against the doorjamb and read aloud, reciting the fact pattern from the case. It was remarkably similar to theirs, unbelievable as that seemed, and Linda's eyes widened as she listened. Finally she got up from her desk and took the book from his hands to read for herself. The judge had ruled in a way favorable to Puritan's viewpoint.

She looked up at him, amazed. He did a quick tap shuffle and ended on one knee with his arms extended like Al Jolson.

Linda laughed out loud and tossed the book in the air. He jumped up, grinning, and picked her up, swinging her by her hands. Jubilant, she planted a loud kiss on his cheek. "You are a genius," she said. As she stepped back, he held her and drew her forward again.

"That peck was not sufficient reward for so spectacular an achievement," he said softly. "I had something more substantial in mind." Before she could move, his mouth came down on hers, hard and sure, impossible to resist. Linda felt her control going. She had wanted him so much, for so long it seemed, and here he was: his mouth, his hands, his body. Her lips opened under his to admit his probing tongue.

The office melted away and the two of them drifted into a separate universe. Linda would never have believed she could feel so strongly. She was dizzy in his arms with the force of her emotion. He smelled wonderful, like soap and starch and with just a hint of tobacco. She pulled her mouth away and pressed it to his neck, moving inside his open collar to touch the springy hairs at the base of his throat. He groaned and cupped the back of her head, encouraging her, his other hand slipping down from her waist to caress and press her to him. Tugging on her hair, he brought her lips up to his again.

The phone on her desk rang loudly, and they sprang apart, like two guilty children caught playing doctor. It was a shrill reminder of the outside world. Linda pressed her hands to her burning cheeks and walked unsteadily to her desk. Out of the corner of her eye she saw Jeff put both palms flat on the wall, his head bowed between his outstretched arms like an athlete trying to catch his breath.

"Linda Redfield," she said into the phone, striving for a normal tone.

"Hi, Linda, it's Maggie."

"Oh, Maggie," Linda said, relieved. What had she expected on the other end, the voice of God?

"Are you all right?"

"Sure, fine. What's up?"

"Well, I tried your house and there was no answer, so I called the office. I'm supposed to be picking you up at six for that lecture at the law school."

Linda sighed. She had forgotten about it completely. "Look, I'll meet you there, okay? I'll go directly from here. If I leave now, I can make it on time."

"See you there. Are you certain nothing's wrong? You sound . . . odd."

"Nothing's wrong. Save me a spot."

Linda hung up and began to throw things into her briefcase, while Jeff watched her with an unreadable expression on his face. After a few moments he said wryly, "It's really not necessary to flee. I'm not going to rape you."

Linda's hands stopped their rapid motion. She decided to confront the issue rather than sidestep it once more. For the first time since the phone rang she looked directly at him.

"It wouldn't be rape, Jeff, and you know it. That's the problem."

He drew a deep breath and held it, as if awaiting what was to come.

She walked around her desk and faced him, noting as always the chiseled features, the direct, clear gaze. She swallowed and plunged ahead.

"Look, Jeff, we've got to stop this. It's going to ruin our working relationship, and this job is important to me. It would be different if something could come of it but . . ."

He stood very still, watching her with intentness she didn't understand. "But?"

She shrugged. "You are involved elsewhere and I have . . . my own interests. So I don't want a cheap, tacky affair that will ultimately damage and jeopardize this chance that I worked so hard to get."

His face closed. "Cheap, tacky. Thanks a lot."

Linda bridled. "Don't put me on the defensive. I can play those games too. You know what I mean."

He unrolled his sleeves briskly, and she realized that he was angry. Momentarily diverted, she said curiously, "You never show anger, do you?"

He inclined his head as if to a compliment. "I was raised to believe that revealing emotion was in bad taste, a bourgeois display, you know." He put his glasses in his pocket and smoothed his hair. "But you obviously find quite a few things about me in bad taste, including my supposed penchant for meaningless liaisons." He glanced back at her, and she was startled to see something like hurt in his eyes. "I keep forgetting that despite our, uh, mutual chemistry, you don't think very much of me."

He left Linda alone in the small office, staring after him into the empty hall.

Linda was distracted all through the lecture. Seated next to her, Maggie made rapid scrawling notes as the speaker, Rutgers Law '65, enthralled the group of law students and practitioners with the intricacies of no-fault divorce. Linda stared unseeingly at a bulletin board announcing a "beer bash" for first-year law students at the St. Germain Student Center Friday night, only to see Jeff's face superimposed on the notice. She was hardly aware that the session had ended, until people around her began filing out, a few stopping to talk with the guest of honor. Maggie tapped her on the shoulder.

"Okay, kiddo, what's going on? You've been orbiting one of Jupiter's moons all evening. I realize that no-fault divorce is hardly a riveting topic, but I get the impression it could have been anyone up there and you would have been just as disconnected."

"I'm just tired, I guess," she said lamely.

Maggie tucked her notebook under her arm and picked up her purse. "It's more than that. Come on, let's get a cup of coffee and you can tell me your tale of woe."

They stopped at a Friendly's just off campus. Linda ordered a grilled cheese sandwich for dinner, which she barely touched. Finally Maggie said, sipping her coffee, "Am I correct in assuming this funk has something to do with Lord Langford, my child?"

Linda nodded miserably.

"Hung up on him, are you?"

Linda raised her eyes to her friend's face. "Does it really show that much?"

Maggie set her cup down. "Only to me. It was the perfect setup. He's pretty irresistible in any case, but for you it was like a moth to the flame. He has a cool, capable air, an almost professorial manner. And you love smarts more than anything, and he's got them in spades. Not to mention the Grecian profile and gorgeous red hair. I swear, do you believe that color? If he were a woman I'd be looking for telltale roots and dye bottles in the trash."

Linda smiled. Maggie could always bring her down to earth. Encouraged by this response, Maggie went on. "I love to watch him play to a jury. In those three-piece suits and those glasses, he looks like that ad for Scotch."

"Last book read: *How to Pick up Girls*," Linda added.

"No, he wrote that one," Maggie said dryly. "Along with *How to Radiate Brains and Breeding from Every Pore* and *How to Look Cool and Composed in 90 Percent Humidity*."

They laughed together, and Linda felt her tension ease. "It's not funny, Maggie. He's coming on to me, and I really want him. It's like a battle every day to hold him off."

Maggie shrugged. "Then why do it? Give in."

"And set myself up for the heartbreak of the century? No, thanks. He probably goes through types like me like Kleenex." Although she said the words, she really didn't believe them. "He'll wind up marrying that blue-blooded Barbie doll and I'll wind up carrying a torch for the rest of my life. He's not forgettable, even from a distance. If I had an affair with him I know what would happen. This is self-preservation time."

"Because, under that high gloss, you think he's really a rat?"

Linda's finger traced a wet circle her cup had left on the formica table. "That's the problem. After working with him, I really don't think that anymore. It would be easier if I could hang onto the prejudice I initially had, but he's actually a nice guy," she finally admitted. "I just know that in the end he'll do the accepted thing and ride off into the sunset with Miss Megabucks or somebody just like her. And I refuse to be an enriching experience along the way."

Maggie signaled the waitress for a refill. "How can you be so sure his attitude toward you is as detached as you seem to think? Something changed your mind about him, right? And why do you think he's pursuing you? I'm sure he can find a more agreeable woman than you have been. Why make the effort to snare one obviously wary and suspicious lady?"

"Availability, maybe. He sees me every day. Perhaps it's the challenge of the elusive. Or maybe..."

Maggie raised her eyebrows. "Well?"

"This probably sounds ridiculous, but I get the impression he's trying to change my opinion of him. He knows I disliked him in the beginning, and he thinks I still do. For some reason it seems to matter to him."

"He probably can't believe there exists a soul who isn't immediately captivated by him, and wants to maintain a perfect score."

"You know, that's what I thought, but I'm not so sure any more. He doesn't seem to have that kind of conceit. It's more like...well, today for example, he was kissing me when you called..."

Maggie's mouth fell open, then closed. "I thought I detected some heavy breathing."

Linda ignored that and continued. "I wanted to leave right away, and he thought it was because I was afraid of him. He was quite bothered by it." She described the scene to Maggie and repeated his comment about Linda not thinking much of him. "And the look on his face," she concluded, "it was as if I'd hurt his feelings."

Maggie studied her friend. "There's a possibility you're not considering here."

"What's that?"

"He may be falling as hard for you as you are for him."

Linda laughed mirthlessly. "This isn't fantasy land, Maggie. I know how I stack up against the women he's used to."

"Why do you put yourself down like that? You don't need me to tell you that you're attractive."

Linda nodded. "And Jeff's Bryn Mawr paramour isn't exactly the Medusa either. And think of all those millions thrown into the bargain. They would add luster to anybody's looks."

Maggie's patience was wearing thin. "But hasn't it occurred to you that he might prefer an intelligent, capable lady who's made her own way to a pedigreed parasite?"

"No, it hasn't, because I'm sure he doesn't see her that way. He comes from that same background himself."

Maggie drained her cup and frowned. "I think you'd better reexamine your thinking, counselor. You're talking out of both sides of your mouth. On the one hand you say he's a good guy, and on the other you say he's such a snob he can only view you as a fleeting diversion. Come on, make up your mind. It may be he has more of a handle on your real feelings than you care to admit. Don't be so sure he's wrong when he says you don't think much of him."

Maggie's words ran through her mind for the rest of the evening, and they were the last thing Linda thought about before she went to sleep.

Chapter Six

LINDA AND JEFF were deep in research in her office when Mary tapped cautiously on Linda's door, then opened it an inch. "I know you told me to hold your calls and take messages, but there's a man named Jesus on the phone, and he insists on talking to you."

"It's a divine message," Jeff said. "Your prayers have been answered."

"I don't think so. Don't you usually *see* somebody, like an angel, or something?" Linda responded in the same vein.

"Maybe not," he replied. "Joan of Arc heard voices."

"Will you take it or not?" Mary asked impatiently.

"Put it through." Linda thought she knew who it was.

Jesus Ortiz has been a client of hers when she was at Legal Aid. She'd represented him when he'd purchased furniture and other household wares under an agreement that renegotiated the contract with each new purchase, leaving an amount due on all purchases, thus never permitting him to pay off any one item. Since the whole lot was subject to repossession if he missed a payment, he'd lost it all when he did just that. Linda had gotten him out of it with an unconscionability, or unfairness, argument, and he had remembered her and tracked her down at her new location.

His problem this time was considerably worse. He was calling from the emergency room at the hospital, where he'd been brought by the police with a stab wound sustained during a barroom brawl. He would be booked on a number of serious charges. He needed a lawyer.

Linda hung up the phone and explained the circumstances rapidly to Jeff. "What do you think?" she asked him. "Would there be any objection to my taking this case?"

Jeff lifted his shoulders. "He could never afford our hourly rate—it would have to be *pro bono*. If you really want to do this, I'll push it through the committee."

"Thanks. He's quite deserving of free representation, I can assure you. Would you mind if we put this off for a while?" She gestured at her cluttered desk. "I'll have to go down there and see what the story is."

Jeff stood, lifting his jacket from the back of his chair. "I'm going with you. I left this afternoon free to work with you on the Puritan thing anyway. Mary can take my calls."

Linda hesitated. She wanted to restrict their time spent together to office hours, and this promised to be a lengthy, unscheduled event. "That's not necessary."

"I think it is," Jeff said firmly. "That hospital is in the worst neighborhood in the city. You're not going down there alone."

Linda found his concern amusing. "Jeff, before I came

to work here, I spent more time in that neighborhood than I did in my living room."

He was not convinced. "Just because you were foolish before does not mean I'll allow you to be foolish now."

This typical male-of-the-species protective reaction from Jeff was a little unexpected, but Linda found, almost to her chagrin, that she liked it. She was so used to looking out for herself that it was nice to let somebody else take charge. It reminded her of her behavior when Bobby had grabbed her at the jail—for a few moments she had acted like a helpless female and welcomed Jeff as her protector.

A frosty wind was blowing as they took the crosstown route to the east side, where the hospital was located. Jeff drove his car while Linda filled him in on the details of Jesus Ortiz's background. It was a history not too different from that of many other Puerto Rican youngsters who had come to this country with their families and high hopes. Jesus' parents could not speak English, the father had had odd jobs, and the mother'd had to try to make ends meet for four children. Jesus was the oldest, and a little better off because he could communicate and had a skill, welding, which he had picked up during summer technical training sessions at the youth center. Linda had a soft spot for him because, unlike many Latino men, who thought women should act subservient and balked at the prospect of a female lawyer, Jesus had always treated her with respect and admiration.

The emergency room was as chaotic as usual, with accident cases, feverish, grubby children, and overdoses. They found Jesus in an examining room, watched over by two uniformed policemen. A harried intern was stitching his arm, which was laid open from the crook of the elbow almost to the wrist. He looked up to see Linda, and his large black eyes lit up.

"Ah, Miss Redfield, thank you so much for coming," he said, eyeing Jeff warily. His accent was faint, almost undiscernible, except in moments of stress, when it became more pronounced. "Who is this with you?"

"Jesus, this is my colleague, Jeff Langford. He works with me at my new job. You can talk in front of him—it's all right."

The two policemen stood by, poker-faced, as Linda got the details of the incident from Jesus. He had been mistaken for another man who had been at the local watering hole earlier. Jesus' opponent was also cut, but not as badly, and had already been treated and taken downtown to be booked. Linda took notes on the witnesses and told Jesus she would talk to the barman and the other patrons who saw the incident, as soon as she could. She made a list of the charges pending after talking with the arresting officer, and assured Jesus that she would do everything possible to help him. He relaxed visibly and had brightened considerably by the time they left.

"Do all your old clients look like him?" Jeff asked, smiling.

"Yes," Linda answered. "And all your old clients look like Cary Grant, right?"

"That's not what I meant," Jeff said. "He's very handsome, and he's got a terrific crush on you."

"He's got a terrific crush on my ability to get him out of this mess," Linda said blandly. "I think that's as far as it goes."

"I don't agree," Jeff said. "He was undressing you right in the examining room. I'm surprised you didn't feel a chill."

Linda let that one pass, aware that if Jeff had noticed Jesus' interest, it must indicate something.

They stopped off at the bar where the fight had taken place and talked to the owner and the bartender. Linda got the names of some of the other customers at the time of the incident, then called it a day.

"They seemed a bit flabbergasted when you said you were representing Jesus," Jeff commented as they emerged into the fading daylight.

"People like us aren't usually too interested in the problems of people like Jesus," Linda said. "You look like an FBI agent, and I look like Miss Muffet. Can you blame them if they seem surprised?"

They walked along Center Street toward the hospital parking lot, where Jeff had left the car. "Do I really look like an FBI agent?" he asked, seeming perturbed.

"Trenchcoat and all." Linda laughed, indicating his double-breasted, belted mackintosh.

"Well, you don't look like Miss Muffet," Jeff spoke with authority. "I can think of several other comparisons, but that isn't one of them."

Linda didn't answer, wondering what he meant. Then she noticed that they were passing one of her favorite lunch spots from her Legal Aid days.

"There's Tony's Pizza," she said. "These are my old stomping grounds, and I can say with conviction that Tony has the best pizza in Springfield."

"That's all I needed to hear," Jeff replied, taking her arm and steering her toward the door. "I love pizza."

"You do?" Linda asked, surprised.

"Sure. It makes for an occasional change from nectar and ambrosia," Jeff replied sarcastically.

Linda followed him in, somewhat abashed. Why did she always let her awareness of the differences between them show so plainly? No matter how hard she tried to think of him as on the same level with herself and others, it didn't work. There was an unbridgeable gulf between them, even if it only existed in her mind.

Once they were seated in a narrow wooden booth, Jeff ordered a small pie and two root beers. "I'll never be able to eat all that," Linda protested.

"I will," Jeff said. "Stick around, I'll amaze you."

Linda was about to say something, when the door opened and Warren Vanders came in. All she needed was for him to humiliate her in front of Jeff. She didn't want to hurt Warren's feelings, she never had, but he was so persistent and so annoying that he brought out the worst in her.

She turned aside, facing the wall, hoping he wouldn't notice her. No such luck. She heard him calling her name and turned stricken eyes to Jeff.

"Who is that?" Jeff asked her, watching Warren's progress toward them with narrowed eyes.

"The bubonic plague," Linda answered. "Or the 1917 flu epidemic—take your pick."

Jeff's lips twitched. "I take it he suffers from unrequited love."

Linda rolled her eyes. "I really don't want to be mean, but I just can't face him after the day I had."

"I'll think of something," Jeff said.

"I suppose it's too late to tell him I died," Linda said darkly, as Warren negotiated the last of the small tables in the center of the room and headed down their aisle.

"Well, hello," Warren said. "I've been looking for you. Then your friend Maggie told me you got a new job."

"That's right," Linda said, smiling pleasantly. Warren's hair stood up in cowlicks, his collar was snapped up under his chin, and his tie was stained. To say that Warren was unkempt was like saying that the Mississippi was a small mountain stream.

He had a personality to match. Linda had accepted

one date with him out of pity, and by the end of the evening she had wanted to hit him with a rock. And to make matters worse, that one evening had encouraged him to the point where he was almost impossible to get rid of. Normal, acceptable people suffered from insecurity and doubts about their social acumen—not Warren. Linda had had to be downright rude to him before he would leave her alone, and suddenly here he was again, turning up like the proverbial bad penny.

"Where are you working now?" Warren asked. Linda pictured him showing up at Rolf, Langford, and Pinney, and her desire for the pizza took a nose dive.

"With me," Jeff said, smiling at Warren. "By the way, congratulations are in order. If you haven't seen Linda, I guess you haven't heard. She was just elected national vice-president of the Gay Lawyers Guild. Isn't that wonderful news?"

Linda choked on her root beer, and Warren's mouth fell open, his eyes becoming as round as billiard balls. Speechless, he stared at Linda, who didn't have too much to say herself.

"We're all very proud of her," Jeff went on smoothly, heedless of his two dumfounded companions. "It's quite an honor."

"Why, uh, yes it...must be," Warren stammered. Then recovering slightly, he went on. "Congratulations, Linda. Well, I have to be going now. I just stopped by to say hello."

He took off the way he'd come, but faster. Jeff watched his retreat, a satisfied grin on his face. "I don't think he'll be bothering you anymore," he said.

"Jeff," Linda gasped, "how could you tell him such an outrageous lie?"

"Look, it got rid of him, didn't it? I told you I'd think of something, and I did."

"Swell," Linda said. "Now he'll be telling that to everyone."

"I doubt it," Jeff replied. "It will only make him look foolish for pursuing you."

After the initial shock, the humor of the situation sank in, and Linda started to laugh. "Did you see his face?" she asked, chuckling.

"Talk· about a picture being worth a thousand words," Jeff said. "I wish I had a shot of his kisser when I delivered that bulletin."

"Maggie calls him Bartleby the Scrivener," Linda informed him. "Just then, he looked more like Bartleby the Stunned."

Their pizza arrived, and Jeff dug in with zest. He gestured to the window behind Linda's head, remarking, "It's started to snow,"

They munched in silence for a while, and then Jeff said, out of the blue, "I understand that you were married."

Linda took a swallow of her soda before replying. "That's right. My husband was killed in a construction accident."

"Were you happy together?" Jeff asked quietly.

Linda thought of giving a conventional answer, but when she looked into his candid green eyes, she found herself blurting out the truth. "No, we weren't."

"Why not?" Jeff inquired, then added, "If it bothers you to talk about it, I understand."

"It doesn't bother me anymore," Linda answered, realizing that it was true. "It used to, but I guess I'm over it."

Jeff waited.

"We were mismatched—got married too young, I suppose," Linda said, sighing. "Jim wanted a different type of woman. He liked the old-fashioned girl, the kind who baked cakes and stitched samplers, and wound up with me instead. I wanted to finish school and have a career. He wanted me to start a family right away. I felt stifled and he felt cheated. If he hadn't died when he did, I don't think the marriage would have lasted much longer."

"It's hard to imagine that any man could be dissatisfied with you," Jeff said.

Linda's hand froze in the act of reaching for a napkin. How could she answer that? "It's sweet of you to say that, but Jim had his own version of the story," Linda answered rapidly, to cover her emotional reaction to his comment. "As his mother constantly pointed out to me, the world is filled with eager young things ready and willing to be just the kind of wife Jim wanted. It wasn't his fault that I didn't fit the bill."

"It sounds like a case of bad judgment on both sides," Jeff remarked.

"It was." Linda toyed with the paper wrapper from her straw. "How did you know I'd been married?"

"Phyllis Beresford told me."

"Phyllis Beresford! That woman must be a reporter in disguise. I'll bet I know where she gets all her information. She cornered me at the Halloween party, but I managed to get away. Still, I think she missed her calling. She would have been a wonderful interrogator."

"She's a barracuda, all right," Jeff said. "I'm convinced she has a network of spies who feed her gossip in exchange for immunity from her probing. She makes me nervous—I always think she's going to whip out a tape recorder and say, 'For the record, Mr. Langford, how many illegitimate children did you say you had living in seclusion under an assumed name?'"

Linda had to laugh at his imitation. He looked and sounded just like her.

Jeff called the waitress and paid the bill. By the time they got outside, it was snowing steadily, and the walk to the parking lot promised to be cold and wet.

"Why don't you wait here, and I'll go get the car," Jeff suggested. "There's no sense in both of us freezing."

Linda stood in the doorway of the restaurant and watched him jog down the street, a dim figure outlined in the neon lights on the corner. It was not long before his car appeared, snowflakes dancing in the illumination provided by the headlights.

"The streets are very slippery," Jeff warned as she got in. "We're going to have to take it slow."

Jeff headed back to the office, where Linda's car was parked, and it soon became apparent that he had not exaggerated the condition of the roads. The BMW shot from one side of the road to the other, like a giant ice skate. No matter how slowly they crawled along, it seemed impossible to maintain control. Linda saw several cars abandoned on the shoulder of the road, their owners apparently having decided that walking was safer. Jeff was a good driver, but it was clear that he was worried.

They had almost made it back to State Street when a car appeared from nowhere, traveling much too fast. Jeff cursed and swerved to avoid it, but it kept coming, skidding in their direction. It was obvious that Jeff could not get out of its way. He let go of the wheel, pulled Linda onto his seat, and jumped on top of her, shielding her with his body. That was the last thing she remembered before the world went black.

Linda woke in the same hospital she had visited that afternoon to see Jesus Ortiz. Though it was nighttime, she could see the nurse's station in the faint light from the corridor and recognized the medicinal smell. A thick gauze bandage was taped to her head, and when she

moved her neck, pain shot through her skull as if it were
being sliced by a knife. She felt weightless, floating, and
knew that she was under the influence of some drug. She
looked around for the call bell and saw a dark shape
looming nearby. Peering fuzzily into the shadows, she
saw Jeff sitting in a chair next to the bed. He was asleep,
his head resting on the edge of the mattress.

She recalled the accident, the sickening crunch of
impact, but little else. She did remember, with a welling
of tenderness for the sleeping figure inches away, how
Jeff had tried to spare her from harm at the last minute.
And what was he still doing here? It must be the middle
of the night, judging by the silence. She moved her
fingers and touched the dense, soft hair. Jeff stirred, then
woke.

Instantly he sat up and snatched her hand, holding it
to his lips. "Darling, you're awake. Are you all right?
Oh, my God, I thought I'd killed you. These doctors
wouldn't tell me anything. I've been so worried, I've
been out of my mind. You looked so small, so still, I
thought surely you were dead. How do you feel? Should
I call the nurse?"

Linda smiled, touching his anxious, drawn face. "I'm
fine," she said groggily, her tongue feeling thick and
fuzzy in her mouth. "My head hurts a little, and I think
I'm floating, but otherwise I'm okay."

Jeff laughed with relief, pressing kisses on her up-
turned palm. Then he bent over the bed, his hands on
either side of her pillow, and kissed her mouth.

"I thought I'd lost you," he murmured. "They were
taking X-rays of your skull. You can't imagine how
scared I was. My lovely Linda," he said huskily, and
kissed her again.

This is a dream, Linda thought. I'm shot full of stuff
and I'm hallucinating. This is what I wish would happen,

and I've got just enough juice in me to think it's real.

Her eyes closed, and Jeff straightened up, whispering, "You'd better rest now, you need the sleep. I'm going to stay right here." He sat back in the chair, drawing it closer to the head of the bed.

"Hold my hand," Linda said to the figment of her imagination, and warm fingers enclosed hers. How about that? An obedient specter.

"Jeff?" she mumbled, drifting off.

"Yes, sweetheart?"

"Can we get another pizza tomorrow?"

Soft laughter floated out of the darkness. "Three. With anchovies, green pepper, the works. Now, go to sleep."

In the morning, Jeff was gone. Had he ever been there? Linda wasn't sure. Her memory of the nighttime waking was so blurred and dreamlike that she could easily believe his presence in her room had been wishful thinking.

A nurse bustled in to give her a shot and examine her pupils. "I see the crazy man has gone home," she remarked.

"Who?"

"The crazy man I heard about from night shift. The guy who was in the car with you. He wouldn't leave even after every doctor on duty had assured him that you would be fine. He insisted on staying in your room. I understand they were going to have him arrested, until they found out that he was Jefferson Langford's son, and then they changed their tune. Old Langford's quite a benefactor around here—they didn't want to get on his bad side."

So Jeff had been there after all.

A doctor showed up a couple of hours later and subjected Linda to some tests, saying finally, "I'd rate you as a pretty lucky young lady. That rap on the head could have been considerably worse, but your friend took the brunt of the impact. It broke a couple of his ribs and two fingers on his left hand."

Linda's eyes filmed with tears. Then what had he been doing sitting up all night with her?

As if reading her mind, the doctor shrugged and said, "He let us tape his ribs and splint the hand, but wouldn't stay for observation. He was ambulatory and conscious, so what could I do? I couldn't keep him against his will. All he was interested in was getting in here to see you. He'd probably still be here, but I persuaded him to go home. I told him that it would upset you to see him sleepless and exhausted." He shook his head. "I wish there were somebody that concerned about me."

Maggie showed up that afternoon, bearing a huge potted plant and a box of chocolates. "What is this?" she asked, peering at Linda, lying in bed. "I always said you'd do anything to get attention."

"It looks worse than it is," Linda replied. "They're going to let me go home tomorrow."

"I take it your hero has departed," Maggie stated. "Reports of his devotion are legendary around here. I gather he went quite bonkers when he thought you might be seriously hurt."

Linda said nothing, but she looked unhappy.

"Well, cheer up, for God's sake, it means that I was right and he does care about you."

"That doesn't change our relative positions."

"Oh, don't start that again. You're going to give me a headache as bad as yours. You're never satisfied, do you know that? First you were miserable because Jim Redfield was an intolerable bully. Now you're miserable because Jeff Langford isn't. What's wrong with your head isn't physical, it's mental."

"That's not true," Linda protested.

"Of course it's true," Maggie snapped. "You've found somebody who appreciates you for what you are, and you have to manufacture other objections to the relationship."

Linda didn't answer.

"All right," Maggie said patiently, "let's take this step by step. He likes the fact that you're intelligent and know how to use your brains, correct?"

Linda nodded. "Just the other day he said to me, 'The nicest thing about you is that you're smart.' Can you imagine Jim's saying something like that?"

"Frankly, I could never imagine Jim's saying anything other than 'Where's my dinner?' or 'How come my shirt isn't ironed?'"

Linda smiled ruefully.

"But you two will never get together, in your opinion, because he's on a higher social plane than you. Don't you see how ridiculous that is? This is America. We have a democracy here. All men are created equal and all of that. The Constitution, Declaration of Independence, remember them? Didn't you go to law school?"

"You can drop the sarcasm, Maggie," Linda said. "You don't understand."

"I understand that you're acting like you're an untouchable and he's the Maharajah of Ranchipur. He's not God, Linda. Why don't you give yourself some credit? It's just possible he's crazy about you, too."

"No it isn't," Linda said stubbornly.

Maggie threw her hands up in surrender. "I give up. I have to go back to work. Water this palm tree when you get a chance. Ignore the snow outside and convince yourself you're in Miami Beach."

"I'll try," Linda said, and Maggie left, shaking her head.

Aunt Marie called from New Jersey. She calmed down after Linda assured her that the injuries were minor. She said that Laurie, Linda's friend from elementary school, had moved to Vermont with her husband and was expecting her second baby. Linda remembered kinetic, outgoing Laurie, a former cheerleader, and tried to picture her snowbound in Bennington with two children. She couldn't do it.

A candy striper came into Linda's room, struggling with a large wicker basket of colorful autumn ferns. The card said, "I'll be back tonight, Jeff."

Shortly thereafter Diana Northrup arrived, in a blue fox jacket and slim tailored slacks, wearing matching kidskin boots and gloves. She removed her fur to reveal an eggshell angora tunic that clung to her slender curves, emphasizing her graceful proportions. Linda wished that Maggie had stayed. She wouldn't think Linda so foolish if she'd gotten a closer look at the competition.

"Jeff told me about the accident," she said in a soft, pleasing voice. "I know he would want me to stop by and see you."

What about what *I* want? Linda thought. She didn't need a visit from her serene highness to really throw her into a depression.

But the marvel of it was that Diana meant well. She could not know the bad effect her appearance was having on the patient she had come to cheer.

They exchanged small talk for a while, and then Diana said, as she was leaving, "I really am happy to see you looking so well. Jeff was very worried about you. He feels responsible because he was driving."

"It wasn't his fault," Linda answered. "I was told that

the driver of the other car was drunk."

"Even so," Diana said. "Jeff is . . . sensitive. He takes things to heart."

Please don't give me a lecture on his fine points, or I may scream, Linda thought. Aloud she said, "Thank you for coming," hoping that would stimulate Diana's exit.

It did. Diana left, leaving the room suffused with her perfume, a reminder of her presence.

That evening the doctor took the dressing from Linda's head and announced that she could be discharged the next day, although she would have to return later to have her stitches removed.

After seeing the doctor, Linda took a shower. She wore a clear plastic cap to protect the wound, and she longed to wash her hair. Maggie had brought her a new bathrobe, and she put that on over the hospital johnny. She did the best she could with the makeup and brush in her purse, and sat up in the straight chair where Jeff had slept on the night of the accident.

Jeff arrived exactly at seven, when visiting hours began. He was dressed in black denim jeans, which made his narrow hips look nonexistent, and a dove-gray sweater. He dropped his pile-lined sheepskin jacket on the bed and sat next to it, leaning forward, with his forearms on his thighs, to study Linda's face.

"You look tired," he said. "Are you getting enough sleep in this place?"

"Jeff, if I slept any more they'd think I was in a coma. That's all I've done since I was brought here. I'm so sick of that bed that when I get out of here I'm not going to close my eyes for a week."

"Well, you're not coming back to work for a while," he insisted. "You need time to recuperate."

"I'm coming back to work on Monday. I've already asked the doctors, and they can't think of a single reason why I should sit around at home, when they can't find anything wrong with me. I'm getting these stitches out in a couple of days and then I'll be as good as new."

"That's the stupidest thing I ever heard."

"Tell that to Dr. Ginotti."

Disgruntled but realizing he was beaten, he changed the subject. "Jesus Ortiz is out on bail," he said. "I arranged it today."

"Thanks, Jeff."

"I think he found me a poor substitute for you," Jeff added. He smiled, but he seemed ill at ease, even shy. Was he regretting the tender scene in this room in the middle of the night? Probably. Now that he was sure there was no danger, he was sorry he'd overreacted. He was no doubt trying to gauge how much she remembered, considering her delirious state.

"Are you sure you're all right?" he persisted after a moment. "I wanted to get a private-duty nurse around the clock for you, but that doctor wouldn't authorize it. He said it wasn't necessary."

"Thank God," Linda said. "If I had woken up to that, I would have been sure I was on my way to my maker."

"I thought you were," Jeff replied. "You were as white as a sheet in the ambulance."

"You rode in the ambulance with me?"

His skin blushed a faint pink. "Well, sure, uh . . . you were unconscious and all. What was I supposed to do?"

"It seems like you've taken very good care of me."

He dropped his eyes. "Isn't that what friends are for?"

Friends. That's telling you, Linda, she said to herself. She didn't need skywriting or neon signs now. She had just heard it from the horse's mouth.

"That's right," she answered.

He lifted his head and met her gaze, his eyes as guile-less as a child's. "We are friends now, aren't we?"

"Of course," Linda said to the man who had called her "darling" and "sweetheart" in that very room.

"I suppose that's something, anyway," he muttered.

Susan Daley arrived, and the talk turned to office matters. When the nurse came around at eight, her visitors left. Linda sat and listened to the final announcement that visiting hours were over, knowing that more than that was over for her.

When she was discharged the next morning, she went to the ward clerk to present her health-insurance cards for billing, and the woman looked at her, puzzled.

"Your bill's already been paid, in full, Ms. Redfield. By that young gentleman, a Mr. Langford. J. Langford, 1227 Williams Street, Longmeadow, Mass."

Linda stood still for a moment, with her wallet in her hand. Oh, Jeff. Why did he keep doing things like this, when she was trying so hard to resist him? He wasn't cooperating at all.

Chapter Seven

WHEN LINDA RETURNED to the office, she was the center of attention for a few hours, as everyone wanted to see the accident victim and assess the damage.

She had had the stitches taken out at the outpatient clinic, and all that remained was an angry red line. In time that would fade to pink, and then to white. Linda began to feel that she should have worn an eye patch or carried a cane, just for dramatic effect, since she didn't look as if she had gone through any ordeal.

Craig asked her to lunch, complaining, as they were seated at the Copper Kettle, that he had missed all the excitement. He'd been out of town on a business trip to Washington when Linda and Jeff had had the accident. He'd just returned the night before, and hadn't found out about it until he arrived at work in the morning.

"But I understand everyone carried on bravely in your absence," Craig said. "Even himself was stalwart, on the job, broken hand and all, dictating into his little machine."

"I hardly expected that business would grind to a halt," Linda replied with a smile. "I've never indulged in delusions of grandeur."

"What's happening with Puritan Petroleum?" Craig asked.

"Jeff pretty much kept up with it," Linda answered, "though it keeps getting complicated. I have dreams about its taking over the world, you know, like the eggplant that ate Chicago."

"It can't be that bad."

"It depends upon what you're comparing it with. Next to some of those patent and antitrust cases, I guess it's small potatoes, but to someone who's been dealing with leases and installment contracts for her entire legal life, it looks like the Rosetta Stone."

Craig snapped a breadstick in half. "Don't worry. Jeffie will bail you out of it. He cut his teeth on cases like that. His moot-court brief at Harvard dealt with the Du Pont merger case. A masterpiece of ingenuity, from what I hear."

"I don't want 'Jeffie' to bail me out of it," Linda replied, with a bit more warmth than she had intended. "If I were the type who waited around for some man to bail me out of difficult situations, I wouldn't be sitting here with you today."

Craig raised his hands in the air in submission. "I apologize. Don't start that feminist stuff with me. I campaigned for the ERA, and I think Gloria Steinem is a modern-day saint. Give me a break, will you?"

"I'm sorry, Craig. I guess I'm a little jumpy today. My desk isn't even visible under the avalanche of paper covering it. I took one look at that mess and wanted to turn right around and go back home to bed. It's funny—

while I was away from it, I missed it and couldn't wait to get back, and when I got back, I wanted to dive under the covers and never look at another subpoena. I can't figure it out."

"That's life, kiddo. Welcome to the human race."

They ordered lunch, and when their salad came, Craig asked, "In the interest of a slight diversion from this humdrum routine, could I persuade you to join me for a small cocktail party Saturday night? One of my former partners bought a new house, and it's a housewarming. They told me I could bring a date. What do you say?"

"Oh, I don't think so, Craig. I have so much to catch up on now that I'll have to jump in on Friday night and not emerge until Monday morning. There are some things that just can't wait any longer. I would have liked to at another time, but not now."

Craig nodded thoughtfully, spearing a cherry tomato with his fork. "That was very gracious, because you are a nice lady. But what you really wanted to say was, 'Give up, there's no magic, and there never will be.'"

"Craig, I—"

"It's all right," he interrupted, "I'm not going to commit suicide or anything. But I'm a pretty bright guy, and I can see which way the wind is blowing. And it's blowing in the direction of Number One Son, is it not?"

"I don't know what you mean."

"I think you do. I hate to be the person to tell you this, but you haven't got a chance. He's all tied up with pink ribbon, baby, and the package has Lady Di's name on it."

Linda said nothing.

"Oh, he wants you, any fool can see that, and why not? But when it comes down to it, he's going to opt for coin of the realm, blue-chip stocks, and Pennsylvania real estate. He's charming and thoughtful and gallant—

I've seen the floor show—but above all he's smart. And he knows where the main chance is. Don't be misled by the pretty manners and the ingenuous air. That is one of the most calculating fellows you'd ever want to meet."

Linda didn't know what to say. He was voicing many of the doubts she had had about Jeff herself, and yet she couldn't help thinking that this was rejection talking. Craig was busily carving up the man he knew she preferred.

"Craig," she said after an uncomfortable pause, "I don't want this to become unpleasant."

"It won't," he said in a friendly tone. "I still like you, and, oddly enough, I like Jeff, though it may be hard to believe after what I just said. Everybody likes Jeff. It's a condition of nature: dogs like bones, kids like toys, and people like Jeff. It's just that I want you to understand where he's coming from. The rich *are* different, Linda. They can't help it. And they stick with their own kind."

"I know what's happening, Craig. You're not saying anything I haven't thought myself."

"That's good to hear. Believe me, I'm not just taking pot shots at my rival. That's no way to win you—it will only make him look better and me look worse. But don't set yourself up for a fall, Linda. I've been here longer than you, and I've seen several others give him their best shot. Jeff isn't deliberately deceptive, he's just"—Craig paused, searching for the right words—"like a kid in a candy store who knows he can have any goody he wants. Do you understand what I'm talking about? He's got too much, and he can't help but use it. I know you think I'm jealous, and to be honest I suppose I am, but it's more than that. I really don't want to see you get hurt."

There was no mistaking his sincerity. "All right, Craig. Thanks for the word to the wise. I'll be careful."

* * *

Jeff had been in court all morning, but he was waiting for her when she got back to the office.

"How do you feel?" he asked anxiously. "Have you had any headaches, dizziness, blurred vision?"

"No symptoms at all."

"Well, that's what Dr. Ginotti said to look for," he said defensively.

"I hate to break this to you, but I have experienced a complete recovery. But I'm glad you're here, because there is something I want to talk to you about. My bill at the hospital was paid before I checked out. It seems a Mr. Langford took care of it. I have a few words to say about that."

"There's nothing to say. The bill is paid. It's done," he said matter-of-factly.

"Jeff, it's not proper!"

He looked at her in amazement and then started to laugh. "Not proper! Linda, this isn't Miss Finch's School for Refined Young Ladies. Proper went out with high-top shoes."

"Not with me, it didn't," she responded.

"Don't I know it," he muttered. "Look, Linda, the firm pays your health insurance as part of your job benefits, right? Well, my father owns the firm, and I will myself one day—part of it, anyway. So look at it as an advance payment out of the same pocket that would have covered your expenses eventually after Blue Cross submitted the bill. This way we cut the red tape and everybody's happy sooner."

"Everybody except me."

He shook his head. "God, are you stubborn. You wouldn't be Irish, by any chance, would you?"

"Welsh."

He grinned. "Same thing."

"Not to a Welshman."

"What was your maiden name?"

"Rees. Linda isn't my real first name, either. It's actually Llhande. My parents Anglicized it to Linda when they came here, because nobody could pronounce it. It means something in Cymric, but I can't remember what."

"Llhande Rees," he said, trying it out.

"Sounds like a stripper, doesn't it?" she remarked, and then, horrified at herself, clamped her mouth shut.

Jeff dissolved in helpless laughter, recovering enough finally to say, "What an improper thing for such a proper young lady to say." He put his hands on her shoulders, one of them bulky from the tape that still bound the broken fingers. "You, my Welsh rarebit, are a delight." he squeezed her, briefly, and then went into his own office, still chuckling.

After their lunch at the Copper Kettle, Craig didn't ask Linda out again. He was still cordial, but it was clear that he had abandoned all efforts to engage her attention.

Later that week Susan Daley stopped Linda in the hall. "Linda, do you mind if I ask you a personal question?"

Linda never knew how to respond when people asked that. What happened if you said, 'Yes, I do mind'?

"What do you want to know?" she asked Susan.

"Are you still seeing Craig Jensen? He asked me out for this weekend, and I don't want to invade your territory."

Linda patted Susan's arm. "Don't give it a second thought, Sue. Craig and I just didn't hit it off. You go ahead with him and have fun."

Susan's face lit up, and she walked away humming. It was considerate of her to ask, Linda thought. Quite a few people she knew would have seized such an opportunity without stopping to worry about anyone else's feelings. Susan was a classy lady. Linda smiled, thinking of Craig's recuperative powers. Good for him. He wasn't one to sit around crying over what he couldn't have. She ought to take a lesson from him.

Maggie came by Linda's house that night to talk her into going on a blind date with her boyfriend, Larry, and a friend from work. The prospect of making conversation with a complete stranger left Linda unmoved.

"Maggie, the last blind date I had was in high school. The guy turned out to be some math genius who was being admitted early to MIT. He spent the whole evening detailing some of his more esoteric theories for me. I don't think I actually fell asleep, but I do recall some rather conspicuous yawning. It did not rank among my premier social experiences."

"So what are you going to do instead, sit home here waiting for Jeff Langford to come riding up on his white charger? I don't know how that's going to happen, since as far as I can tell from what you've said, you haven't given the guy a clue as to how you feel about him. Is he supposed to be telepathic, or what?"

"Maggie, we've been all through this. I was hoping you had broken that record."

"I'm going to play it just one more time. You're crazy about him, but he doesn't know it. You don't want him to know it, because he's out of your league and he already has what you consider to be an appropriate mate waiting in the wings to be trotted out when the time is right. Meanwhile, you refuse to even consider seeing someone else, because no one could possibly measure up to the unattainable Mr. L. Honey, I don't want to be downbeat about this, but it sounds to me like you have an insoluble problem."

"I know that." Linda's voice was so forlorn that Maggie was alarmed. She sat on Linda's wing chair and studied her friend's face. She had known Linda for a long time, and had never seen her look quite so defeated. Linda was one of the most resourceful people she knew. It was hard to believe that this situation had totally unnerved her.

"I wonder what would happen if I called Jeff and had a little talk with him myself," Maggie said thoughtfully.

"Maggie, I love you, but if you do that, I will kill you," Linda responded quietly.

"So what's going to happen?" Maggie inquired. "Are you going to become a recluse and take up knitting? Are you going to write secret, passionate poetry and stuff the papers in drawers, like Emily Dickinson? Or are you going to go serenely insane, like the Brontës? Which is it to be? I want to be prepared."

"Maggie, stop being so dramatic. I know I'm not the first woman to find herself in this situation." Linda sighed. "Others have survived, and so will I."

"I'm not so sure about that. You're acting pretty damned peculiar, and I don't like it."

"I'm not too happy about it myself."

Maggie straightened and folded her hands in her lap. "Look, Linda, I know it hurts. I've been there. But don't let it spoil your chances for finding somebody else. If I had your looks and brains, I wouldn't be doing anagrams with Larry. You threw away Craig Jensen, who's clever and cute and now happily chasing Susan, who won't make your mistake, if I read my cards correctly. I can think of others, too many, who've been wrong for you for this or that trifling reason. And I remember some you couldn't even give a reason for not liking. Has it occurred to you that you only want what you think you cannot have?"

Linda sighed and folded her arms. "Thank you, Dr.

Hilton. Where did you get your psychiatric degree?"

"I'm just trying to be logical," Maggie said grumpily.

"Logical! If I could apply logic to my feelings for Jeff, I wouldn't be in this fix. I wish I could reason or diagram it away, but every morning when I wake up it's still there, that dull ache that says, you want him but you can't have him."

"I wish I could help you," Maggie said softly.

"I wish you could too," Linda replied, and meant it.

Winter took a cold grip on western New England and wouldn't let go. The weather turned fierce; subzero temperatures and bone-chilling winds kept all but the hardiest troopers indoors. The skies were leaden and theatening all the time, but little snow actually fell. The news services started carrying reports of people frozen to death in their unheated homes. Linda stopped listening. Was it all as depressing as it seemed to her, or was it her mood?

She buried herself in her work, and it kept her busy enough to put thoughts of Jeff in the background. When she saw him at the office, she kept all conversations short and to the point. Maggie still badgered her to get out and be active in order to forget her troubles, but it seemed pointless to Linda. She had never been an escape artist, had never learned the fine art of forgetting problems by partying or going to boisterous gatherings. She always remembered what was bothering her. It was the price she paid for her steel-trap mind: the trap closed around her when she desired most to be free.

Jeff called her on her intercom several weeks after their accident to say that the driver of the car that had hit them was being prosecuted for driving under the influence, driving to endanger, and a number of other violations. He seemed to think she would be pleased at this news, but it had little effect. Tales of another's misfortune did not erase her own.

That evening she emerged from the office to see Jeff getting into Diana's Audi 5000. His car was still being repaired, as foreign parts were hard to obtain. Linda watched them drive off and thought how odd life was, that these two people she hadn't even known a short time ago should now command so much of her attention. As much as she tried to dismiss them, they reappeared, in dreams at night as well as in the daylight hours. She even had a nightmare. Jeff and Diana were safe on shore watching her drown. They were laughing and refused to throw her a lifeline. Freud would have had a ball with that one, Linda thought.

Linda was the last one left at the office one Friday afternoon, or so she thought until Jeff appeared in her doorway to beg a ride home.

"Isn't Diana giving you a lift?" Linda asked neutrally.

"She went to Boston early for the weekend," Jeff explained. "I couldn't see the point of renting a car for one day."

"Call a cab," Linda said heartlessly. She wanted to be in his company as little as possible.

He thought she was kidding. "You'd make me ride home in a cab? An injured man in my condition?"

"Your ribs are healed, and those two little ace bandages on your fingers hardly qualify you as the walking wounded," Linda answered.

He looked quizzically at her, and Linda realized just how rude she was being. "Okay," she conceded, "just let me get my stuff together, and I'll be right with you."

It was already dark when they left, and the city streets were clogged with traffic. Linda tried to think of a good topic of conversation, but she was so afraid of saying something that would give her feelings away that she restricted her comments to banalities and monosyllabic replies to his questions.

When they pulled up to Jeff's house, Linda didn't shut the motor off, intending to let him out, then keep going. He reached over and shut the motor off for her, taking her keys. Her heart sank, and she almost cried with frustration. What now?

"Come in for a minute," Jeff said. "I have something for you."

"Jeff, can't you bring whatever it is to work on Monday? I really don't have the time and—"

"This won't wait until Monday. It will only take a minute."

Filled with misgivings, she followed him up the porch steps and into the front hall. He snapped on the overhead light and led the way into the living room.

"Da-da," he said, making a sweeping gesture toward a small end table beside the couch. On it sat a chocolate cake, inscribed in white icing with the words, "Happy Birthday Llhande."

"Did I spell it right?" he asked.

"You spelled it right," Linda whispered. "How did you know?"

"Your birthdate was on your résumé," he answered. "I made a note of it."

He waited for her to say something more, and when she didn't, he misinterpreted her silence. "Bad idea, huh? I wanted to get you a gift, but I knew you wouldn't accept anything from me. So this seemed like a . . . well, I'm sorry if I did the wrong thing."

She shook her head, still too stunned to speak. He took her by the shoulders and turned her around to face him, his face full of concern.

"Linda, what is it? I didn't mean to upset you."

She put her hand to her mouth, her distress so obvious that he put his arms around her.

"Baby, don't," he murmured, "don't look like that. I only wanted to please you."

Every resolution she had made about their situation went out the window once she was in his arms, where she had longed to be so many times. He stroked her hair and rocked her, finally taking her hands and pulling her onto a love seat with him, cradling her in his lap.

"Tell me," he said. "Tell me what I've done."

She put her hand to his lips to silence him, and he said, "Let lips do what hands do," and kissed her.

What feeble resistance she had managed to build up fled in an instant before an onslaught of passion so devastating that it drove all rational thought from her mind. He kissed her until her lips were bruised and raw, his hands moving everywhere, burning through her clothes. He eased her down until she was lying full length under him, his body urgent and demanding against hers. It wasn't enough, and with a guttural sound of dissatisfaction he sat up, drawing her with him, bending her body over his arm like a bow.

"I want to touch you," he said huskily. "Take these off."

Clinging as if drugged, she let him strip her, gasping when his mouth covered her breast through the thin cloth of her slip. He ran his hand along her leg, her thigh, and Linda was powerless to stop him. When he released her for a moment to shed his own clothes, she watched, dazed, eager for his return. Then her glance fell on a framed photo of Diana on the mahogany sideboard. She had not seen it the last time she was here.

Moaning, she sat up, clutching her slip to her half-exposed breasts. She couldn't look at him.

Jeff heard the sound and fell to his knees beside her.

"What's the matter?" he asked, trying to take her in his arms again. She was unyielding, paralyzed with humiliation. He let her go abruptly, standing up and running his hands through his disordered hair.

"Linda, don't do this to me—not when I've wanted you so badly and waited so long."

She didn't answer, but merely folded her arms across her midriff and bent forward. He watched her, saw the pain, and relented.

"All right," he said. "Put your clothes on." He turned his back as she dressed herself, trying to calm himself down.

Linda was in shock, and couldn't seem to make her fingers work. She left her blouse unbuttoned, and her coat hung open as she got up to leave.

He whirled when he heard her moving toward the door, and stopped her. "You can't go like that," he said, "you'll freeze to death."

Obediently she fastened everything that needed fastening. She seemed to come to when he said, "I want you to know I didn't have this in mind when I asked you for a ride. I just wanted to surprise you with the cake, and then things got out of hand."

Linda seized his arm, her eyes wide. "Promise me," she said. "Promise me."

He shook her off, staring at her as if she were a stranger. "Promise you what? That I won't want to make love to you again?" His voice was agonized. "How can I promise you that?"

"Promise me that you won't try it again," Linda replied. "Or else I'll have to quit my job. I can't take any more of this."

"You drive a hard bargain, lady," he said bitterly. "Having you around but not being able to touch you, or not having you around at all."

"Please," she whispered. "We have to work together, and I won't be able to handle it if I think something like this might happen again."

"Was it so terrible?" he asked tonelessly. "Am I that repulsive?"

"Oh, Jeff, you know that isn't it. You're anything but repulsive. That's the whole problem. Can we go back to the way we were before—colleagues—or do I have to leave the firm?"

"Given the choice, what do you expect me to say? You're probably doing me a favor. I think I've had enough torture at your hands. Rest assured, I won't bother you again."

And he didn't. On Monday Linda waited, nervously, for him to give some sign, some indication, of what had occurred on Friday night. But he had regained his equanimity, and she gradually relaxed. It was is if it had never happened. And she was thankful, for she had another pressing problem.

Chapter Eight

LINDA COULD HARDLY believe that the preliminary hearing on the Puritan case was scheduled for the next morning. It seemed that they had been working on it since the dawn of time, eating and sleeping it, and it still wasn't completely ready. She and Jeff stayed long after the others had gone, to finish up. They finally broke for something to eat at ten o'clock, when it became apparent that it was going to be hours before they could even think of going home.

Jeff returned with a bag of burgers and two coffees. As he removed the wrappings he commented, "The nutritionists say this is pretty revolting stuff, but supposedly there are 26 trillion, or some equally ridiculous number, sold, so they must be doing something right."

Linda bit into a satisfying mouthful and said, "I was raised on them. My aunt used to say that if I ever got sick they'd have to be liquefied and fed to me intravenously." She wiped her mouth with a napkin. "I suppose you were more used to filet mignon when you were growing up."

He stopped chewing. "When I was growing up," he said shortly, "I was used to eating with the servants in the kitchen. As a result, I developed a passion for soul food that endures to this day."

He obviously considered the subject closed, and Linda didn't probe. He continued to glance through his note cards as he ate, and wadded the greasy paper without looking at it. She watched him stand and stretch, the taut fabric of his oxford-cloth shirt emphasizing the breadth of his shoulders and the narrowness of his waist. He pitched the ball into the basket by the door. "Two points," he said.

He pulled the plastic lid off his cup, leaning against his desk and crossing his legs at the ankle. His bleached and faded jeans fit him like a second skin, molding the long slender muscles of his thighs. Linda drew her gaze away, wishing suddenly that he had not changed for the racquetball game that afternoon. He was a lot easier to resist in his Ivy League camouflage—not that he looked less attractive in it, but it made him appear more remote, less approachable.

Her thoughts were interrupted by his voice calling, "Heads up." A shiny silver object shot through the air toward her, and she caught it reflexively. It was a candy bar wrapped in foil. "Sweets to the sweet," he said, extracting another from his back pocket.

"Thank you, Hamlet."

"You're welcome, Ophelia. This offering is guaranteed to rot your teeth and induce diabetes."

"So kind of you to think of me. Where did you find these?"

"In the vending machine downstairs," he said through a mouthful of chocolate. "Instant energy."

"Well, I could sure use some of that."

He carried his cup back to the conference table where they had been working. "Come on, we've not yet begun to fight."

Linda nodded. "Back to the salt mines."

They worked for several hours more. When Linda looked at her watch again it was 2:30 A.M.

"Jeff, I'm done. My handwriting is doing a snake dance before my eyes. If we don't quit now, I'll die right here, and the cleaning lady will find my body in the morning."

He rubbed his eyes. "It is the morning. All right, I'm worn out too. Let's just leave everything where it is, and we'll pick up where we left off. The hearing isn't until eleven, so we'll have a couple of hours more to put in on it."

He left the room and came back with his down jacket and her camel's-hair coat. He pulled her wool hat out of one sleeve and jammed it over her ears, extracting her mittens from the other and drawing them on her hands. "Some hot shot," he mumbled under his breath. "Can't even dress herself."

Linda was too tired to respond. She propped herself against the wall while he zipped zippers and snapped snaps. "That thing should have a combination," she said, nodding to his jacket.

"Very amusing," he replied. "At least it's warm."

The elevators were off, so they walked down the five flights of stairs in companionable silence. Once outside, the cold of the winter night cut into them like a razor slicing through their clothes.

"God, it's freezing. Let's run," Jeff said, breaking into a trot and dragging Linda along with him.

Their cars were the only two left in the lot. He jogged in place next to her door as she fit her key into the ignition with numbed fingers. The only response was a series of clicks. The battery was dead.

Linda put her hands on the steering wheel and stared at it with weary resignation. "I should have known this would happen," she groaned. "It's been starting badly all week, and I guess this cold killed it. It's usually in the garage at night."

"Leave it," he said, his breath frosty in the stinging air. "We'll jump it or get it towed in the morning. I'll drop you at home."

They bundled into Jeff's BMW, which warmed up quickly. Linda's townhouse was only a short distance away, but she knew Jeff would have to drive to the highway to get to Longmeadow. He looked as if he were about to pass out, and as they pulled up to her door she said, "Come in for a minute. I'll make you some instant coffee so you can stay awake long enough to get home."

He hesitated a moment, and it seemed to Linda that he was trying to read her face in the dim glow of the street lamp above them. Then he shut off the motor. "Thanks." He followed her up the brick walk to the small porch and stamped his feet while she unlocked the door.

Once inside, he made straight for the couch in the living room. "I'll just stretch out here for a minute while you get the coffee," he said.

In the kitchen, Linda put the kettle on. She took out the coffee, a mug, milk, and sugar and put them on a tray. While waiting for the water to boil, she folded a linen napkin and put it with a spoon next to the cup. She mixed the hot water with the instant coffee, then carried the tray into the living room.

Jeff was fast asleep on the sofa, still wearing his coat and shoes. He looked like a little boy, with his head pillowed on one arm, and the sight of him filled her with an aching tenderness.

She could not bear to disturb him. She felt his exhaustion herself. She set the tray down on an end table and took her mother's afghan from the cedar chest under the bay window. She drew it over him and turned out the light.

In her bedroom she undressed quickly in the dark and pulled on the nightgown hanging on the back of the door. As she climbed into bed she thought of Jeff sleeping in the next room, and happiness enclosed her like a pleasant dream.

Linda was awakened by a dark figure in the hall outside her bedroom. She was momentarily frightened, and it took her a few seconds to orient herself and remember what had happened.

"I'm sorry I woke you," Jeff whispered. "I was going to leave you a note when I left."

"What time is it?" Linda asked, yawning.

"Nine. I think your mailman at the box roused me."

"Nine in the morning?" Linda exclaimed, sitting up in bed. They were both late.

"Relax," Jeff said from the doorway. "I already called the office and told Mary that I was meeting with a client this morning, and to reschedule my appointments. I also told her I had sent you out of town on research. I'll go in later so they won't think it's suspicious that we're...uh...out together. So stay home today. You could use the rest."

Linda was touched by his thoughtfulness. "Thank you."

"I'll call Judge Keady today and get an extension. We're just not going to be able to finish the brief on time, and not for lack of trying. I'm usually prompt with him, so I'm sure he'll be reasonable."

"Okay."

"I'll just take a shower and go, if that's all right."

"Sure. There are some clean towels in the linen closet in the bathroom. And there's soap and a new toothbrush, too, I think."

He lingered a moment longer, looking at her huddled under the covers, almost invisible in the negligible light admitted by the closed drapes. She in turn could make out nothing more than his shadowy outline. The day must be very dark.

"I'll let myself out," he said. "Go back to sleep." He shut her door.

Linda lay in bed, her mind racing with images of him in the shower. It was impossible to sleep. She listened to the rush of water in the pipes and tried to absorb the fact that Jefferson Langford was standing naked not twenty feet away, behind the wall. Feeling restless, she decided to get up and make him some coffee and see if he wanted something to eat before he left.

Climbing out of bed, she pulled back the curtains and saw why the light was so dim. It was sleeting heavily, with the sky a gunmetal gray, and traffic moved at a snail's pace. Neighbors without garages were hacking away at the thin, stubborn coat of ice that obscured their windshields and froze their locks. New England! Linda thought, making a face. On a day like this she would cheerfully give it back to Squanto, Massasoit, or whoever had held it originally. She was glad she would not have to drive in this weather.

She heard the water shut off in the bathroom. She realized that she needed her robe and then remembered that it was in the laundry basket in the cellar. She went to retrieve it, and the bathroom door opened just as she was going past it.

Jeff stopped short, and they confronted each other. He wore nothing but a towel wrapped around his waist, and was pushing his wet hair back with his hands. When he saw her standing inches from him, he closed his eyes.

"I thought I told you to go back to sleep," he said, slowly and distinctly.

"I know, but I decided to make some coffee and..." Her sentence trailed off as his honey lashes lifted again and they stared at each other. In defense, she dropped her gaze, and found herself staring at his body.

Clothing made him look thinner than he actually was. She knew from experience his effortless strength, saw now the flat belly ribbed with muscle, the firm ropy arms and shoulders, the sculptured torso. Droplets still glistened on his skin, and dampness darkened his golden hair to bronze. God, he was beautiful.

His eyes moved over her, in the gossamer nightgown, taking in the firm roundness of her breasts and hips, the creamy skin exposed by the brief top of her nightwear. Desire grew between them like a palpable thing. Linda felt it singing through her veins, beating in her blood, and filling her with the urge to touch. She saw the answering need in his face.

He reached out for her, wordlessly, and she stepped into his arms. Her face was pressed against the smooth skin of his shoulder, a contrast with the tough tissue beneath. His hands molded her to him through the gauzy material. He shifted his stance to take her weight, and his towel fell to the floor. She felt him, stallion-ready, against her thighs.

"So soft," he murmured in her ear. "Like velvet, all over." She traced the taut muscles of his back, and they contracted at her slightest touch. He pulled her even closer to him, and she lifted her lips to his.

His kiss was gentle and exploring at first, but quickly became demanding. They fused together until she thought she would faint with the sensation. Linda's head fell back as his mouth traveled to her throat, and he whispered, "Come to bed with me."

Hearing it brought her out of the mist for a second, and she drew away from him slightly. Instantly he tightened his grip, his voice low and urgent above her. "Please."

She heard that one word and was lost. She loved him; it seemed there had never been a time when she didn't love him. This chance would not come again. She turned back to him, and he guided her into her room, her head on his shoulder, his arm around her. When she reached to pull the curtains closed, he stayed her. "Leave them," he said. "I want to see you."

They stood next to the bed as he slipped the straps off her shoulders and pushed the gown to her waist. His eyes were luminous in the pearly light. He caressed her gently, repeatedly, until she sagged against him, her knees too weak to support her. She heard the swift intake of his breath when her bare flesh touched his.

With a single movement he slid the gown off of her and put her on the bed. He knelt beside her on the floor and crushed his face against her breasts. "Lovely Linda," he said hoarsely. She sank her hands into the profusion of russet hair as his mouth traveled down her body, teasing her into an intimate contact that made him moan aloud. She reached to pull him on top of her, not caring about anything except the craving within her to have him totally. As he enfolded her in the ultimate embrace he said against her lips, "Love?" and she answered simply, "Yes."

Linda wakened in an empty bed. Dusk had fallen, and the light from the hall cast a pool of yellow on the rug. She smiled and stretched, remembering the day.

Getting out of bed, she picked up her nightgown from its tangle in the sheets and slipped it on. As she raised her arm over her head, she could smell the scent of Jeff's soap. With her tongue, she tasted him on her lips.

Yawning, she wandered to the kitchen and put the kettle on, recalling the turn of events since the last time she had done so. The clock said 5:10. She had no idea when he had left—she hoped he had managed to get to the office, as he'd planned.

She opened the front door to get the paper, wrapped in its protective plastic bag. As she sat down at the table she found a single red rose on her place mat, with a folded sheet ripped from her phone pad. When she opened the paper, she saw in flowing script, "Merci. Jeff."

Linda sat with the flower in her hands, moved by the gesture. Where on earth had he managed to get the blossom in the middle of a storm? What a courtly thing to do. He was a real gentleman, no doubt about it. Finally, she set it aside and unfolded the newspaper.

A picture on the first page of the society section caught her eye. Jeff was grinning into the camera, looking like Tom Sawyer about to outfox Aunt Polly. A radiant Diana Northrup clung to his arm. The caption read, "Northrup Heiress to Wed."

Frozen, she continued to read.

Mr. and Mrs. Carter Northrup of Gladwyne, Pennsylvania, and Bar Harbor, Maine, have announced the engagement of their daughter, Diana Augusta, to Mr. Jefferson Tillman Langford III, son of Jefferson Langford II, of Boston. The future groom is a partner of the firm founded by his grandfather, Rolf, Langford, and Pinney. Mr. Langford is a former Assistant District Attorney for the city of Boston and . . .

Linda's eyes moved rapidly over the story, which

outlined the couple's education and family history. She read it so many times that she had it almost memorized, the last line remaining etched in her mind. "A Christmas wedding is planned." She refolded the paper carefully and mechanically got up to turn off the gas under the screeching kettle.

Of course, you idiot, what did you expect? she said to herself. Did you actually think that today meant anything to him? She sat down once more and remained motionless for some time, lost in thought. Then she got up again to throw the paper and the rose in the garbage.

The next morning Linda decided on a course of action while getting dressed for work. She had never really imagined that she could look for anything permanent with Jeff, but yesterday, bathed in the afterglow of their love-making, she had dared to hope for some kind of relationship. Now that she knew his plans, she was certainly not going to carry on an affair with a man getting married in a month. She would convince him that she was treating the episode as casually as he obviously was, and would manage to finish working with him as gracefully as possible.

Linda was not a woman who customarily lied to herself, and she was not going to start now. She loved him, but her pride dictated that he think her as free-spirited as himself. For one brief moment as she brushed her teeth she heard his voice, tense with longing, asking "Love?" and her whispered answer, "Yes." Then she caught sight of herself in the mirror over the sink and said, "Fool!" to her reflection through a mouthful of green foam. People in such intimate situations said things they didn't mean. It happened all the time.

During the drive to work she summoned all the logic drummed into her by her legal training and marshaled it to help herself. She was standing in the reception area, talking to Mary, when Jeff arrived. The sight of him almost made her falter, but she steeled herself. She had dealt with law school, the bar exam, hostile witnesses, and angry judges. She would deal with this.

Mary broke into a huge smile. "Well, Mr. Langford. Congratulations. I saw your engagement announcement in the paper."

Jeff, looking alarmed, turned to face Linda. "Yes," she added calmly. "I saw the paper too. Congratulations."

He darted a quick look at Mary, taking Linda by the arm and ushering her into her office. "Hold all my calls. I'll be in conference with Ms. Redfield if anybody wants me." He pulled the door shut behind them.

As soon as they were alone he said rapidly, "Linda, I want to explain about that announcement. . . . I'm not engaged."

Linda stared at him. "What do you mean, you're not engaged? Were Mary and I, and everyone else who read that newspaper, having a hallucination?"

He looked overwhelmed at the prospect of trying to make her understand. "It was a mistake. Diana and I talked about getting engaged at Thanksgiving, and her mother knew we had discussed it. I guess she must have released the announcement to the press without checking with us." He looked at Linda pointedly. "I've changed my mind recently. I no longer want to marry Diana."

And what am I supposed to do in response to that statement? Linda thought, still smarting from the hurt she'd felt the night before. Throw myself at his feet? Absolutely not.

"Perhaps you're making a mistake," Linda said sweetly. "Diana is a beautiful, cultured girl, who would probably make you very happy."

Jeff examined her, unable to believe her polite, disinterested reaction. He must be wondering what happened to the woman who had yielded to him as if she could never get close enough, crying out his name at the height of her passion, clinging to him afterward, her face wet with tears. She's vanished forever, thanks to your game playing, mister, Linda thought. She left a changeling in her place, this distant, withdrawn stranger. Me.

"I thought...after yesterday..." he began uncertainly.

"What about yesterday? Look, Jeff, we're both adults. It was pleasant, and we both enjoyed it. Didn't you?"

He looked away, seemingly unable to deal with her controlled, rational expression. He focused on her diplomas on the wall. "You know I did," he said quietly.

"I'm glad. Then there's no harm done, and we can go on as before."

Jeff was looking at her with a strange expression on his face. Why is he doing that? Linda thought, confused herself by the bewilderment and pain she thought she saw in his eyes. Did he really think that I would let him seesaw back and forth between me and Diana, whether they were engaged or not? The very fact that they had come that close to such a commitment put him off limits for Linda. He could never have been serious about his relationship with Linda if he was keeping Diana on the back burner. It was just as she had thought all along—Linda could be a one-night stand, but Diana was for keeps.

"*Can* we go on as before?" Jeff asked softly, still looking at her as if she had stabbed him.

"I intend to," Linda said lightly. To change the subject she added, "The newspaper said that you were supposed to get married at Christmas. Why the hurry?"

He shot her a glance, suddenly alert. Linda realized

that the sharpness of the comment was too revealing, and immediately softened her tone. "But I guess there was no reason to wait, right? Take action once the decision is made—I'm for that," she added brightly.

His eyes met hers, his face now blank. "I'm sure you are," he said evenly. "But there won't be any wedding. I'll call you later about putting the Puritan brief together."

"Fine." Linda waited until he was gone before trusting her coordination. Noticing that her hands were shaking, she sat and folded them on her desk. Linda, she mused, if that scene were on film, you'd be this year's winner of the Academy Award.

The Christmas party for the County Bar Association was that weekend. Linda could not imagine feeling less social, but knew that she should at least make a token appearance for the sake of her career. She chose an ice-blue off-the-shoulder cocktail dress that made the most of her eyes and her pale complexion. Sweeping her hair up into a chignon, she fastened it with a jeweled clip and added matching earrings. A silver purse and shoes completed the outfit. Examining herself in the mirror before leaving her house, she was satisfied that she did not look like she was pining away for the youngest partner of Rolf, Langford, and Pinney. It was a good thing that those attending the gathering couldn't read minds.

The affair was held in the main room of the Hampden Country Club. It was richly decorated for Christmas, though it was only early December. Enamel bowls of holly, the leaves and berries misted lightly, sat on every banquet table. Large evergreen wreaths, frosted white and decorated with bells and bows of red and gold, hung on the walls. A huge tree stood on an elevated dais in one corner, reaching to the ceiling and giving off its unique delightful smell. White lights, like miniature can-

dles, glowed amongst its branches, and glittering deco-
rations bent the boughs with their weight. The whole
effect was one of overwhelming holiday cheer. It struck
a hollow note with Linda.

She sat at the firm's table and ate the benefit dinner,
interspersed with music from the four-piece band. She
danced with the senior partners, made conversation with
their wives, and chatted with her coworkers. She watched
everyone get livelier as the evening progressed, and
wished that she were somewhere else. The festive atmosphere only contributed to the depression that had
begun when she sighted Jeff and Diana at the other end
of the table. Diana looked gorgeous in a cherry silk
shantung that intensified her porcelain blondness. Jeff's
dark tuxedo and ruffled shirt set off his patrician looks
perfectly. Together, they drew admiring glances, like
celebrities on a night out.

Linda was busy calculating the earliest possible time
that she could make a graceful exit, when she saw Diana
dance past with Howard Pinney. A moment later Jeff
appeared behind her chair and asked her to dance.

He's only asking to be polite, Linda told herself as
she stepped into his arms. Because his date is dancing
with someone else. But his hand on her bare back, the
sturdy feel of his spine under her fingers, called up images that she was trying to forget. He said nothing, but
steered her expertly across the floor to the open doors at
the rear of the banquet room. Beyond was a small entry
hall. He stepped into it and, holding her by the hand,
pulled her after him.

"Look up," he said softly. A sprig of mistletoe hung
from a fixture in the ceiling. She resisted, but he held
her fast. "It's customary," he said, his eyes mysterious
in the flickering light. Her heart drumming, Linda stood
still.

Jeff bent his head and kissed her. His lips were cool and fresh, tasting of the wine he had drunk. The touch of them was light and fleeting, for he pulled back to see her face, his hands still gripping hers. In the background, the band played, "I'll Be Home for Christmas."

Linda was amazed at her calmness. She resolved to betray none of the emotion she felt at his closeness. She could act casual too.

He searched her face, seeming to be waiting for some reaction. She looked up at him without expression. "You'd better get back," Linda said quietly. "Diana is probably looking for you."

Her remark had the desired effect. Jeff dropped her hands and turned away, but instead of walking back into the banquet room, he continued through the hall, past the hat-check girl, and went outside into the frosty December night.

Curious, she followed and stood by the window of the entry. Jeff stopped next to one of the decorative lanterns that flanked the steps and lit a cigarette. Linda thought that he must be freezing without his overcoat, but he seemed impervious to the temperature, thoughtfully blowing smoke streams into the air. Was he bothered, preoccupied, or was she searching for evidence of something that did not exist? As she watched, he lit a second cigarette from the stub of the first, tossing the old butt away. He sat on the cold stone, propping his elbows on his knees and thrusting his hands into his hair. Then he slowly folded his arms and let his head fall onto them, the cigarette burning away unnoticed between his fingers. His posture so clearly indicated unhappiness, perhaps even despair, that Linda had to resist the strong impulse to run outside, to go to him. But why did he need comforting? What was he feeling? He was so guarded around other people that she knew he would never indulge in such behavior if he thought himself observed. The easy patter and the offhand style were a cover, but for what? He certainly was not the image of a successful, cheerful young man right now. While Linda had to admit to a base feeling of pleasure at this realization, she loved him enough to wish him well on whatever course he chose. She wanted his happiness, even if it was happiness in which she did not share.

He must have been lost in thought, because she saw him start as some ash fell on his pants. He heaved a heavy sigh and took a last drag, then crushed the stub under his shoe. He stood and put his hands into his pockets, then walked slowly back toward the Club. Linda left the window and slipped back into the crowd.

Chapter Nine

A FEW DAYS after the Bar Association party, Mary buzzed Linda's office at about three o'clock. Linda was just reviewing the file on a client she would see in a few minutes, and she was distracted and only half listening when she answered.

"Yes?"

"Ms. Redfield, Mr. Langford asked me to inform you that Mr. Gentry of Puritan Petroleum wishes the two of you to be his guests this weekend. Since you have those depositions to take, he felt that you could see the contracts administrator and the marketing representative on Friday, then be his dinner companions Friday night. He will be sending the Lear Jet to Wilbraham to pick you up, and it will take you to Logan. He's booking you rooms for Friday and Saturday night at the Dempsey House, at the company's expense. The plane will be waiting at the airfield at 10:00 A.M. on Friday. If these arrangements are satisfactory, Mr. Langford will confirm them. If there is a problem, please let him know immediately."

Stunned, Linda sat with her finger on the intercom switch. She'd known they were going to Boston on Friday for the depositions, but she had envisioned driving up and back in the same day, not this whirlwind social schedule complete with private jet and hotel accommodations. This was certainly going to ruin her plans to avoid Jeff as much as possible.

But what could she do? Puritan was one of the firm's top clients. She couldn't risk offending Gentry by spurning his generosity. She had to go—she knew the case better than anyone, and Jeff would need her to help him.

"Mary, please tell Mr. Langford that those arrangements are satisfactory," she said, groaning inwardly. She felt cowardly asking Mary to talk to Jeff, but just hearing his voice was enough to stir up her emotions these days.

Linda spent the rest of the week keeping as busy as possible, so she wouldn't have to think about what was coming. On Thursday afternoon, Jeff stopped her in the hall.

"Is everything ready for tomorrow?" he asked.

"I have the interrogatories prepared, and the statements for each of them to sign. I presume you have the rest."

He nodded, watching her closely. They had been very careful with each other since the events of the previous week, both finding it hard to resume the light banter of their earlier relationship after what had passed between them.

"Linda, I want you to know that I won't take advantage of this...er...development to pressure you into something you don't want. You've made it very clear how you feel about me, or I guess I should say how you don't feel, so you can relax. Let's just try to get through this as gracefully as possible. I want to avoid an uncomfortable situation with Gentry, so it will be best if we act normally and get the job done."

Linda said, "Of course," wondering how she was supposed to act normally under these circumstances.

On Thursday night she packed a bag, including an aqua silk dress for Friday's dinner as well as the usual skirts and jackets for her business meetings. As an afterthought, she threw in a pair of jeans and her Weejun loafers. She shut the case with the feeling that she was sealing her doom inside it as well as her clothes.

Friday morning was bright and cold. She and Jeff took a taxi to the private airfield in suburban Wilbraham, where the Gentry jet was waiting. They were in Boston in forty-five minutes.

At the elegant Dempsey House, Linda was alarmed to find that they had adjacent rooms, 412 and 414. They signed the register and followed the bellhop into the elevator.

Linda's room was beautiful, decorated in gold and white, with thick cream carpeting and a gilt-edged bedspread offset by accents of deep blue in the covering of the loveseat by the window and the paintings on the walls. There was a huge bouquet of yellow roses on a table by the door. The card was signed, "Walter Gentry." She was certainly getting the red-carpet treatment, she thought as she turned away from the flowers. They reminded her of the afternoon of the storm at her townhouse with Jeff, and it was a memory she was seeking to bury, not revive.

She left her bag unpacked on the floor; they were due at Puritan in a few minutes, and she didn't have time to dawdle. She turned to find Jeff lounging in her doorway.

She jumped, and he closed his eyes. "Will you please stop doing that, Linda?" he asked quietly.

"What?"

"Leaping three feet into the air every time you see me

or I speak to you. Anyone would think, from the way you're acting, that I had brutalized you."

But you have, she cried inwardly. He had brutalized her feelings, by making her fall hopelessly in love with him even when he was busy dangling someone else along. Didn't he realize what it was like seeing him every day, imagining him with her, imagining the long lonely nights ahead without him? It would have been so much easier if she had never known what it was like with him; she would have wondered always, but never been sure. Now she was. Sure that it would never be that . . . transcendant with anyone else again.

These thoughts raced through her mind as she looked back at him, managing to say coolly, "I don't know what you're talking about, Jeff." She picked up her purse and breezed past him out the door, leaving him no choice but to follow.

She stopped in the lobby, telling him that she wanted to freshen up in the powder room. She needed a few minutes to compose herself. This was proving to be even more difficult than she had imagined.

She looked at herself in the ornate mirror in the waiting room, where several wealthy matrons sat at the dressing table applying makeup and arranging their hair. Linda stood behind them and examined her tan plaid jacket and brown knife-pleated skirt, the bone cowl-neck sweater, and the matching brown wool vest. She was wearing the outfit of a competent professional woman, which was what she had considered herself . . . until she met Jefferson Langford. Now she felt like a child masquerading in her mother's clothes. Who would believe that someone who looked so intelligent could be so stupid? Linda believed it. She turned away, leaving the Back Bay ladies to their chatter.

Jeff was seated in one of the chairs in the central lounge, waiting for her. He had opened his navy cashmere overcoat to reveal a lightweight wool suit in a color like pale toast, with a sea-green tie and a shirt of lighter, but similar, shade. His Phi Beta Kappa key hung from his vest. Isn't that wonderful, Linda thought wryly, our clothes are harmonious. Too bad our lives aren't.

He handed her her double-breasted Chesterfield coat in silence. She buttoned it, following him outside, where he had a cab waiting. She felt too close to him sitting in the back seat, and he noticed it when she moved away from him toward the door. He turned his head and looked out the window.

They drove southeast of the Common into the business district, where the streets, which had once been cowpaths, were narrow and winding. The home offices of Puritan Petroleum were on Tremont Street, and they turned off Washington to reach it. Jeff paid the driver, and they entered once more the arena of money and influence they had left behind at Rolf, Langford, and Pinney.

Puritan Petroleum, and its employees, exuded the same quiet air of understated affluence that prevailed at Jeff's grandfather's firm. Linda reflected once more that she might never have seen this side of life if it hadn't been for the man now walking beside her. She glanced at him. His expression was closed, thoughtful. That was nothing new.

Walter Gentry welcomed them with that special brand of cultured hospitality one is trained to from birth in the upper classes, in which the person being made welcome feels it an honor and a privilege to be included in the welcomer's range of acquaintances. Coffee was served to them by a stunningly beautiful redhead, who eyed Jeff covertly as she handed around the Lenox china cups. The service was pewter, the cream real, fresh and delicious. It appeared that no expense was spared at Puritan Petroleum.

"So this is the lovely Ms. Redfield I've been hearing about. It's so uplifting to meet a young lady who is as bright as she is beautiful," Gentry said.

This comment did not go over very well with the redhead. She was too well trained to react visibly, but Linda thought she detected a certain stiffening of the spine. In retribution, she glanced at Jeff and smiled dazzlingly. Linda wanted to kick her.

Gentry waited until the amenities were over and the girl had left, before he said, "Well, shall we begin? I have Mrs. Gathrid and John Hobson waiting for you. I understand you will be deposing both of them today?"

Jeff nodded. "We'll get the statements witnessed, and notarize them later. We want to make certain that all the information is accurate. We can't afford to be ill prepared on this one."

Gentry nodded, pleased. "I agree. I've made the conference rooms available to you today. If you want anything at all, send for Stacey. When you would like lunch, just let her know. She can send out for whatever you like, or she can make a reservation for you now, if you wish. Just put the bill on Puritan's account. We have an account at all the major restaurants."

I'm sure you do, Linda thought dryly. She heard Jeff say that they would prefer to stay in and not be distracted. Speak for yourself, she wanted to scream at him. I can use all the distraction I can get.

Gentry beamed at them. "Fine, fine. I'll look forward to seeing you tonight. My car will pick you up at the Dempsey at eight."

Linda followed Jeff down a sleek, paneled hallway to a suite of adjoining conference rooms. They were dec-

orated in hushed tones of celery and peach, with Au-
busson rugs and silk draperies complemented by
Waterford crystal chandeliers and dark oak furniture.
Each contained a huge oval central table flanked by twelve
chairs. Linda repaired to one with John Hobson, the
contracts administrator, while Jeff went to another with
the middle-aged Mrs. Gathrid, the marketing representative.

Linda was exhausted by the time the day's business
was completed. The work was extremely painstaking:
questions and answers had to be phrased very carefully,
so as not to leave any loopholes or openings for the
opposition to leap into and create a chasm. John Hobson
was cooperative; he had an accurate memory for detail,
which really aided the process. He was about Jeff's age,
a stocky, dark-haired ex-football player, who'd gone to
college on a scholarship. Linda recognized a kindred
spirit. When he asked her out to dinner for that evening,
she wished that she could go.

She left with Jeff at six o'clock, and John walked
them out to the elevator. "I'm taking a rain check on that
dinner," he said meaningfully to Linda. "Let's try to
make it tomorrow."

Jeff's eyes flashed to her face as they descended to
the street. "What was that all about?"

"He asked me out to dinner tonight, and I told him I
couldn't go."

Jeff's mouth tightened. "You didn't waste much time,
did you? First Craig, and now John Hobson. He's divorced, you know, one of the most notorious lechers in
the Northeast."

"It takes one to know one," Linda snapped, and his
face showed the impact of the arrow when it struck home.
Oh, God, Linda thought, I'm lowering myself to the level
of children's taunts. Pretty soon I'll be telling him that

his mother wears army boots. It should have been funny, but it wasn't.

He was still wearing a wounded look. For some reason, this only enraged Linda further. "I noticed you're still escorting your nonfiancée all over the map. You'd better tell *her* you're not marrying her."

"I have," he said quietly.

"But she's still hanging in there, hoping you'll change your mind. How flattering. She must consider you quite a prize package."

He set his jaw but did not answer.

"And of course her devotion keeps you from getting *too* lonely," she sneered.

Jeff's mouth hardened. "What am I supposed to do, join a monastery? *You*'ve hardly spoken to me since that damned, blighted, Godforsaken announcement appeared." He extended a hand, palm up, in a gesture of appeal. "I explained that that was an error, Linda. What else can I say?"

"And once I heard that explanation, you expected me to go running after you." She looked away. "You never felt anything for me. You were just amusing yourself, the way you're amusing yourself with Diana right now. Both of us fed your ego, in different ways."

He stared at her, seemingly stunned. "If you really think that, there's nothing I can do. You honestly believe we could have shared what we did with no real feeling between us." He shook his head.

"What did we share?" Linda asked cruelly. "A roll in the hay. That should be nothing new for you, Casanova."

"So you're just giving up," he said heatedly. "A good lawyer always knows when to dig in for a fight, counselor. What's the matter? No killer instinct?" He was giving her back her own bitter medicine.

"I only fight when there's something worth fighting

for," she retorted nastily. "You didn't prepare your brief properly, Mr. Attorney, or you would have known I'd never become involved with an engaged man."

"I . . . was . . . never . . . engaged," he said through gritted teeth, biting off each word individually, firing each one at her as if it were a bullet.

"There is insufficient evidence to support your claim," Linda answered. "The decision has been handed down, and the case is closed. There is no appeal."

He nodded slowly, his face blank. "All right, your honor," he said quietly. "I beg the court's indulgence. I meant no disrespect. I don't agree with the verdict, but I will try to accept it."

"Succeed," Linda snapped, "because that's the way it's going into the books."

Jeff hailed a cab, and they rode back to the hotel in grim silence.

When they reached the Dempsey, Linda went straight to her room to bathe and change. Jeff left her in the lobby and headed for the bar, where she saw him order a drink and light a cigarette. He's tense, she thought, remembering what he'd said the evening of Bobby's attack on her at the police station. And Linda knew she was the cause. She couldn't seem to restrain herself from behaving like a perfect witch. He was probably dreading the night ahead, wondering whether she would make a scene in front of his firm's biggest client. She felt sorry for him and ashamed of herself.

She dressed slowly, selecting her accessories with care. She wanted to make a nice impression, for Jeff's sake. She resolved to apologize to him and be as pleasant as possible that evening. It wouldn't kill her to be civil for one night, no matter how miserable she actually was.

The silk dress she donned was an iridescent blend of

shimmering shades of blue and green, with bands of
alternating opaque and solid material. It was to be worn
over a skimpy chemise of darker hue, strapless and clinging. The total effect was subtly sexy, intriguing rather
than revealing. Black slender-heeled sandals would expose her feet to the cold, but the impact of them was too
striking to be denied. They went well with the gray-
tinted nylons she had selected, which flattered her legs.
Linda surveyed her image in the full-length mirror on
the back of the door and was satisfied.

She debated about the style of her hair. She usually
wore it down, or tied back, at work. Jeff had never seen
it in a fancier arrangement. She fussed with it, not sure
what to do. She finally coiled it into a loose topknot,
leaving tendrils to escape at the sides, to soften the style.
She inserted her only pair of diamond studs in her ears
and put her opal necklace around her throat, where it lay
gleaming with milky intensity. She used a little more
makeup than usual: eye shadow as well as mascara, a
darker shade of blusher and lipstick. She took out the
tiny bottle of perfume she reserved for special occasions
and sprayed it in the air, then walked through the mist,
feeling it cling to her diaphanous dress. She was ready.

Jeff knocked on her door at five minutes to eight.
When she opened it he studied her wordlessly, his eyes
moving over her from head to foot. She waited for him
to speak, but he said nothing.

The pause gave her a chance to examine him. He was
wearing a white dinner jacket with black piping, teamed
with narrow black pants with a satin stripe down the
sides. His shirt was blue, with tiny ribbed tucks all down
the front, topped by a black satin bowtie.

"Aren't you going to say anything?" she asked him
softly.

"You are more beautiful than I can believe," he answered, taking his arm from behind his back and handing her a florist's box. Under the saffron cellophane cover was a single dewy orchid on a bed of tissue paper.

Linda took it from him, biting her lip hard in an effort to control her emotions. After her horrid behavior this afternoon, he had ordered this for her. She deserved a spanking, not a gift. She didn't know what to do.

She walked slowly over to the mirror and put the flower in her hair, fastening it with a hairpin. The task gave her a minute to get herself in hand and think about what to say.

She turned to face him, waiting for her on the threshold.

"Jeff, I'm sorry for the way I behaved today. You're right, we should be mature about this and make the best of the situation. I think we can have a good time tonight, if we try, don't you?"

His eyes became lambent, and he smiled gently. "Yes, I do. I could hardly have a bad time with so exquisite a companion."

He always knew what was the right thing to say. It was just one of the many things about him that she loved; he never missed a cue or flubbed a line. And if he didn't know what to say, he kept silent, a virtue to be treasured in anyone.

He held out his arm to her, and she took it, smiling up into his handsome face. My dear, my dear, it is not so dreadful here, she said to herself, repeating the admonition to Persephone in hell. She was in a hell of her own making, where the torment would be the eternal deprivation of the man she loved. But for tonight, he was with her, and she would have to be thankful for small favors.

* * *

Walter Gentry's house was just off Scollay Square on
Beacon Hill, a restored 1800's mansion that rose in brick
and marble splendor. It had been designed by Charles
Bulfinch, and had a view of the gold dome of the Massachusetts State House. A Mercedes 450 SL sports car
and a Rolls Silver Cloud stood under the archway by the
service entry. Garages, which could be seen in the distance around a bend in the path, had obviously been built
after the main house.

A uniformed butler met them at the door, taking their
wraps and leading them into a richly appointed study,
where a fire burned in the hearth of a magnificent fireplace inlaid with imported tile. Portraits of Gentry ancestors covered the walls.

They were served drinks and canapes by a housemaid,
while Mrs. Gentry, a conservatively dressed handsome
woman in her fifties, made light conversation. Their host
appeared after a few minutes, looking apologetic.

"I'm sorry, my boy," he said to Jeff, "but the demands
of business kept me. I will turn it all over to my son one
of these days, but that date never seems to arrive." He
smiled ingratiatingly at Linda. "And the lovely Linda, I
may call you that, mayn't I? That's what your name
means in Spanish, my dear, lovely. And you are very
linda," he said, giving the word its Hispanic pronunci-
ation. "If I didn't know young Langford here was all
business, I might suspect that his interest in you was
more than academic."

That comment fell into an awful silence. Recovering
first, Jeff said smoothly, "My father sends his regards,
Walter. He said to tell you he's been meaning to call
you about a golf game one of these days. The Club hasn't
seen you in quite a while."

"Oh, that old devil, trying to take me for every penny

I'm worth. You never saw anyone cheat like this one's dad. Why, I remember..." And he was off on an assortment of old-duffer stories that took them through to dinner.

The dining room was off the wide center hall, across from the main salon. It was furnished in priceless cherry Chippendale pieces. The Chinese rug was a magnificent tapestry of dragons in a Ming design, enhanced by the taupe brocade window hangings. The table was set with Royal Doulton china and Towle sterling flatware, both vintage and rare. The Yugoslavian crystal flashed prisms of fire from its etched facings. Linda tried not to stare, but she had never seen anything so beautiful in her life. Jeff might be used to this, but she wasn't, and it was an effort to act as if she ate in such surroundings every day.

The polished brass chandelier added to the soft light cast by a candelabra in the center of the table. The napkins and tablecloth were of finest damask, and Linda almost hesitated to use the linen, it was so beautiful. The dinner began with soup, followed by duckling in orange sauce and a vinaigrette of vegetables. It was all delicious. The dessert mousse was so thick and sweet that it cloyed after a few spoonfuls.

Linda talked mostly to Mrs. Gentry during the meal, while Jeff discussed old family friends with her husband. Mrs. Gentry's children were grown, and she devoted most of her time to charities. An hour of talking to her dispelled quite a few of Linda's illusions about the idle rich. The woman seemed to devote herself tirelessly to the welfare of those less fortunate than herself, and Linda found her an interesting and admirable dinner companion.

They relaxed in a small, plant-filled solarium while they drank coffee and liqueurs. Linda was shown Mrs. Gentry's prize blooms in a greenhouse that was attached to the main house by a covered walkway. They returned to find Jeff and Mr. Gentry laughing together over a joke. When he saw Linda, Mr. Gentry said, "Ah, it does my heart good to see this fellow again. I've known him ever since he was a little shaver."

"Little is the operative word," Jeff said dryly.

"Oh, shush," Mrs. Gentry said. "This one was always convinced he was a midget."

"I was five foot four until I was sixteen years old," Jeff said. "When I played basketball, I passed the ball through the other guys' legs."

"Nonsense," she said firmly.

"I was short, Clara."

"That situation has certainly changed," Linda commented.

"Everything comes to him who waits," Jeff replied, grinning. Linda watched him, her heart expanding with love. She didn't realize how her face was revealing what she was feeling, until she saw Mrs. Gentry studying her intently, a concerned frown wrinkling her brow. Watch it, Linda, she told herself. You're giving yourself away.

They left the Gentrys' at eleven thirty and were back at the Dempsey at midnight. Jeff took Linda up to the fourth floor, standing uncertainly in the hall as she unlocked her door.

"Will you be visiting your family while you're here?" Linda asked, not wanting to part company with him, stalling shamelessly.

"No. My father is in Europe, and my two sisters are married, with families of their own. There is nobody here for me."

"What about your mother?"

"She isn't here either," he answered shortly.

"What's on the agenda for tomorrow?"

"I think we can finish up at Puritan in the morning, and we'll have the afternoon free. Maybe you'll want to do some shopping in town while you're here. I'll be going out to Diana's house in Brookline. You're welcome to join me if you'd like."

Linda felt the smile freeze on her face. Was he serious? He seemed to be, standing there looking down at her, his face totally impassive.

"I don't think so, Jeff. Thanks anyway."

He seemed to come to a decision. "Look, I'm too keyed up to sleep. Would you like to go downstairs for a while? There's usually a lot going on after hours here, and I need to wind down."

And I need to get away from you before I make a complete fool of myself, she thought. "No, I'm tired. I'm going to turn in. I'll see you in the morning."

He nodded, and seemed about to turn away. Then he took her chin in his hand and gazed deep into her eyes. "I'm glad we made a truce. I sure didn't like having you mad at me."

Then his hand fell away and he was gone.

She had certainly done it now. This had probably been her last chance to be alone with him, and she'd said no. She was angry with herself for wanting to go with him and angry with herself for turning him down.

Irritated beyond bearing with her own weakness, Linda unpacked her overnight case in a blaze of fury, flinging lingerie and street clothes onto the bed and the floor in a multicolored blizzard. Feeling slightly better after this emotional outburst, she realized that she was thirsty. She called down to the desk for soda and some ice. A few minutes later there was a knock at the door. Thinking that it was the bellhop with her order, she flung the door open.

It was Jeff.

She sighed resignedly. "Jeff, you just left. What are you doing back here?"

"I'm sleepwalking. Care to join me?"

She couldn't take much more of this. Why didn't he just go away and leave her alone? The stress of his constant company, of having to be on her guard every moment, was driving her mad.

"It's almost 1:00 A.M. We have work to do tomorrow. I'm going to get some sleep, and I suggest that you do the same."

"Forget it. As that old saying goes, 'I'll sleep when I'm dead.' After careful consideration, I decided to reissue my invitation to join me for a little early-bird entertainment. Or night-owl entertainment, depending on your point of view."

"Jeff, I'm not dressed," she said, pointing to her robe, though the excuse sounded feeble even to her. She knew that she wanted to be with him more than anything. Her last futile defenses were crumbling.

"That's ridiculous," he said, walking into the room. "Here, this is nice. Put it on."

Linda closed her eyes. "Jeff, that is a nightgown."

"Oh," he said, dropping it back onto the bed, "so it is. Well, something else, then. Anything." He paused, taking in the disorder. "That is, if you can find it. It's quite an amazing mess here, madam."

"I quite agree, sir—the results of a trifling fit of temper."

He leaned back against the hotel dresser, his palms flat on its polished surface. "Something is upsetting you, isn't it, Linda?"

Nothing to speak of, she thought. I'm pointlessly in love with you, trying to resist being added to your doll collection, and I'm trapped in this darling little weekend jaunt that has me practically living with you. "Just tired, I guess. Long week, long weekend," she explained.

He pushed himself up, spreading his hands. "I rest my case. What you need is some relaxation. If you're not downstairs in the lobby in fifteen minutes, I am staging a *raid* on this room."

He smiled villainously, twirling an imaginary mustache, and vanished, whistling.

Linda sat on the edge of the bed. He wasn't taking no for an answer, and of course she really wanted to go. She was just afraid of what would happen if she did. The last thing she needed was another sample of what she would be missing for the rest of her life.

Then she stood up, shrugged, and unbelted her robe. She would live dangerously. For one night she would follow her feelings, since this might be the last time she would ever do so.

She rummaged in the tossed salad of her clothes and came up with the jeans she'd added at the last minute, and a tailored blouse. She brushed her hair and pulled it back in a tortoise-shell clip, adding a touch of fresh makeup. Glancing in the mirror, she had to smile. She looked like a bobby soxer on her way to a movie.

Jeff was dressed in khakis, with a striped woven belt and a forest Lacoste shirt that turned his eyes the elusive gray-green of Connemara marble. Leaning on the reception desk with his elbows, smoking, he brought to mind Evelyn Waugh's "magically beautiful youth," Sebastian Flyte, waiting to board the train for Oxford.

"Come with me," he said when he saw her, extending his hand. "I want to show you something."

On the first floor, to the rear of the banquet hall and restaurant, there was a game room. The sound of video games and clicking, ringing pinball machines could be heard as they approached.

"I'll bet you didn't know I was a pinball wizard," he said slyly, inclining his head toward her as if sharing a great mystery.

"Truthfully, I did not."

He nodded and winked, putting a finger to his lips. "It's the best-kept secret in Springfield. Bad for the corporate image." He dropped coins in a machine and waggled his hands loosely, like a swimmer in the starting blocks shaking down. Then he stepped up to it, knees braced, fingers clamped on the controls, and the machine exploded with noise and light.

He soon drew onlookers. He seemed to become one with the machine, rocking to its rhythm, manipulating the handles with lightning speed. Linda stood by, watching in amazement. He rode it the way a cowboy rode a bucking horse, whooping and hollering, slamming his weight against it as if he could dominate it with sheer physical strength.

Watching him play, Linda felt such tenderness welling inside her that it was akin to pain. She had never seen him having such a good time. He looked about half his age, a slender, agile teenager pitting reflexes and cleverness against electronic gadgetry. When he stopped, the group around him applauded.

He walked over to Linda, triumphant, rotating an upraised hand in the air slowly, like a model in a hand-lotion commercial.

"Such a subtle wrist," he said, laughing.

"Wherever did you learn to do that?"

"When I was in law school, I spent more time in the pizza joints on Massachusetts Ave than I did in the library. It stays with you, like riding a bicycle."

"May I try?" Linda asked.

He was delighted. "Sure. I'm through showing off for tonight."

She took up the position that he had had, and to her alarm, he stood directly behind her, his hands over hers on the controls. She was acutely aware of his presence, of his body pressing lightly against her back.

"Now, the object of this game," he said solemnly, "is to keep those little devils up on top by hitting them with the levers. You can't let them drop to the well at the bottom." He demonstrated, showing her how to do it.

Linda was too distracted by his nearness to really concentrate, but she tried, and he rewarded her efforts with a kiss on the back of her neck. Her heart racing, she slipped out of his embrace.

"I'm sorry," he said immediately. "I know I'm breaking the terms of the treaty. I promised to keep things innocent and friendly. Have one drink with me to show me I'm forgiven."

Knowing that it was a mistake, Linda went with him to the small bar next door, where a three-piece band played in a dimly lit corner. A few couples were dancing to slow numbers.

"I don't suppose you'd dance with me," he said.

"You suppose correctly," she answered lightly.

They sat nursing their drinks, Linda torn between the feeling that she should get up and leave, and the desire to stay with him at all costs. The beat of the music quickened, and a younger, more energetic group took over the floor. Linda watched them gyrating to the vocalist's rendition of a pop hit.

A pretty brown-haired girl of about eighteen, wearing incredibly tight satin slacks and a low-cut bolero top, walked over to their table. "Wanna get down?" she said to Jeff, smiling.

"Can you do that?" Linda asked archly, nodding toward the dance floor.

"Can I do that? Can Katharine Hepburn act? Can

Heifetz play the violin? Can Sugar Ray Leonard box?"
With an "I'll show you" look to Linda, he took the
brunette's hand and followed her onto the dance floor.

He could do it. Fingers snapping, torso twisting, hips
rotating to the primitive beat, he leaned into his partner,
giving the girl more excitement in minutes than she'd
probably had in the last few years of fending off the
advances of high-school Romeos. Linda watched for as
long as she could stand it, but he looked so good,
so . . . sexy, that her low tolerance snapped and she put
down her drink, unable to take any more of it. Knowing
that she was behaving badly but past caring, she dashed
from the bar. He didn't seem to notice that she'd gone.

Back in her room, she lay down on the bed and stared
at the ceiling, too drained to cry. You are the best-ed-
ucated idiot in the state of Massachusetts, Linda Redfield, she told herself. You knew this was coming and
you let it happen anyway.

It was not long before she heard Jeff pounding on her
door. "Linda, let me in."

"Go away," she yelled.

"Open this door, or I swear I will go downstairs and
tell the desk clerk some lie and get him to open it for
me."

Wearily, she unlocked it, to see him standing in the
hall, breathing heavily, his shirt and hair damp from his
recent exertions.

"Why did you leave like that?" he demanded. "I thought
you were waiting for me, and when I got back to the
table you were gone."

"I'm surprised you missed me, you were having such
a great time," she said bitterly. "What happened to Miss
Teenage America? Did you wear her out?"

He looked bewildered. "What are you talking about? We were just dancing."

"Just dancing! Yeah, you and Salome, just dancing." John the Baptist's head, and my heart, she added silently.

He looked totally exasperated. "Linda, what is wrong with you?"

"What's wrong with me is you!" she replied, almost screaming at him. "Being so nice, looking so . . . so . . ." She gestured, her hand taking him in from head to foot, at a loss for words. "Making me want you so, when I can't have you," she added helplessly, admitting finally what she had sworn never to let him know.

His face changed instantly, and he rushed toward her. "Darling, here I am, you can have me. You always could."

"No," she said desperately, raising her hands to fend him off, "no." She was unable to detail her objections any further.

"Yes, damn it, yes," he insisted, gritting his teeth, catching her wrists in an iron grip, not hurting but holding her fast. He pushed her against the wall, crushing her between it and his body. "Feel me, darling. Remember? Can't you let go, Linda, and give us what we both need?"

Against her will, almost without volition, her hands crept to his waist, inside the shirt, and moved up his spine, caressing the skin, still slick with perspiration. Moaning, she pressed her lips to the soft flesh at the base of his throat.

It was all the invitation he required. Stepping away from her for a second, he pulled the shirt over his head, tossing it on the floor. He pulled her back into his arms immediately. She tasted his damp, salty chest and shoulders, rubbing her nose in the bristly mat of coppery hair roughening his breast. With a low sound of impatience, he raised her lips to his, twining his fingers in her hair to hold her steady for his plundering of her mouth. She hung onto him, too weak to stand on her own, letting him carry her for what she knew would be the last time.

He cupped an arm under her knees and lifted her onto the bed with him, taking off her things. "These buttons are multiplying," he ground out in frustration, finally yanking on the blouse and sending the last three flying in separate arcs. Heedless, he nuzzled her, unhooking the bra she wore with a nimble thumb and forefinger. He pulled the lacy garment from her body, and her breasts sprang free. Almost before he saw it, he had a pebble-hard nipple in his mouth, a groan of satisfaction emanating from deep in his throat.

Linda held the golden head against her, luxuriating in the feel of him, every nerve in her body on fire. His tongue rasped against her swollen flesh, and she arched her back in abandoned response. Gradually his mouth moved lower, across the silken skin of her belly and thighs, ever more intimate, until she shuddered silently, inarticulate with pleasure. She tried to raise him up to her, to embrace him, but he continued to caress her until she was ready, ready, more than ready, whimpering in her demand for fulfillment. He removed his remaining clothes in seconds.

When at last he moved over her, she clasped him close, running her fingers over his back and shoulders, delighting in the taut muscles, rigid with sexual tension. She threw her head back as he buried his flushed face in the curve of her neck, gripping her hips, lifting them to meet his entry. She gasped at the contact, and he raised his head, looking into her eyes, his own filled with tender reproach.

"Why did you deny us this?" he murmured. "Why?"

Unable to answer for the tightness in her throat, she gazed at the beloved face, inches from hers. This is for remembrance, she thought, and gave herself up to the ancient rhythms, as old as time.

Linda woke at dawn, to find Jeff sleeping with his head pillowed on her breast. Carefully, so as not to wake him, she slipped out from under his weight, taking her robe from the foot of the bed. She stood by the window and watched day breaking over Boston.

They had loved many times during the night. How easy it had been to forget their true situation, to pretend that her ardent, tender lover would be hers forever. But morning came, as it always did, and brought brutal truth with the sunlight. She took her eyes from the skyline and turned back to the room, where she stumbled over Jeff's clothes on the rug.

She picked up his slacks, and a slip of paper fell out of his pocket. It was a message from the desk clerk for Jeff, dated last night while they had been at the Gentrys'. She knew she shouldn't read it. She did anyway.

"Ms. Northrup will meet you at the travel agency at 1:00 P.M. Saturday. She has planned luncheon with her parents after the business there is concluded."

So he was going to see a travel agent today with Diana. To plan a romantic shared vacation, no doubt. And he had had the nerve to ask Linda along for the luncheon, when he'd be coming straight from examining brochures about the Caribbean love nests where he would wine and dine his lovely companion.

Linda crumpled the slip of paper in her hand and threw it in the wastebasket. Fool me once, shame on you, fool me twice, shame on me. Trite but accurate. She had been fooled twice, had allowed herself to be. No more. This was the end of the line.

Firm in her resolve, she showered quickly and dressed quietly, making sure she did not rouse the sleeping man.

She threw her things together into the bag, and was ready to go in minutes. With a final glance at the bright head on the pillow, she slipped out the door.

She had an early breakfast in the hotel restaurant, then turned in her room key. She would not be needing it any longer.

Linda had arranged to meet John Hobson at the Puritan offices at nine, and she was there waiting for him when he arrived. Since it was not a regular working day, there were few people around. He unlocked a conference room and prepared to settle in.

"John, would you mind terribly if we went somewhere else? It would be so much nicer if we could relax away from these corporate surroundings, don't you think?"

He went for the bait, as she had known he would. Jeff was due to see Mrs. Gathrid shortly, and she wanted to be gone when he arrived.

Linda left a note for Jeff on Mrs. Gathrid's desk, sure he would find it when they set to work. "I'll be finishing up with John this morning, and I will take a commercial flight back to Springfield this afternoon. Won't be staying to see the Gentrys tonight. Will make my apologies to Mrs. Gentry personally. Have a good time at the Northrups' today. See you at the office. Linda."

Let him make of that what he would.

Linda made short work of the rest of her business with John, who was disappointed when he found she would not stay for dinner that night. He wanted to take her to Anthony's Pier, a famous seafood restaurant on the bay, but Linda was afraid she just might jump in.

She had never felt so overwhelmed with despair and loneliness. Walking out of the Bar Association library, where they had gone to wind up the depositions, she listened to John's small talk while the scene last night in her hotel room replayed itself in her mind like a video tape. She kept seeing Jeff's face above her, the thick, curling lashes, the sensitive, mobile mouth. She shook her head. Enough of that.

She had telephoned from the Bar library and booked herself on a flight back to Springfield at 2:00, scheduled to land at Bradley field at 2:45. She excused herself from lunching with John but allowed him to drive her to the Gentrys', where she intended to make an excuse for that evening. She knew she should have called first, but was afraid that Mrs. Gentry would talk her into staying. Her excuse would be more convincing if presented in person, Linda thought.

When he dropped her off, John tried to get her to commit herself to a date the next weekend, but she sidestepped him, asking him to call her on Wednesday. She didn't want to go anywhere with him, but she didn't have the nerve to refuse him again, when he had been so nice to her.

The butler showed her into the study, and as she waited for Mrs. Gentry, Linda wondered whether Jeff had been planning to bring Diana to the little soiree they were supposed to attend that night. That would have made a charming group—perhaps he was even considering inviting a date for Linda, just to keep things congenial. She wished Mr. Gentry had never made his spontaneous invitation when they were leaving the night before. It made this stop necessary, and she wanted to put Boston behind her as quickly as possible.

Mrs. Gentry entered, the embodiment of graciousness. "My dear, how nice to see you earlier than expected. My husband and I are so looking forward to your company again this evening."

"Actually, Mrs. Gentry, that's why I'm here. I won't be able to come this evening, and I wanted to tell you in person. You and your husband have both been so kind to me, I felt I should stop off before I left and let you know."

"So you will not be flying back with Jefferson?"

Even his name produced an unwanted response, and Mrs. Gentry, who missed nothing, saw it.

"No. I'm going back this afternoon, on my own."

"Is there something in Springfield calling you back early?"

"No, nothing like that. I just thought I'd like some extra time to go over the depositions before we present them in court on Monday."

Mrs. Gentry nodded, and signaled the housemaid to bring some tea. She examined Linda, her keen intelligence reflected in her china-blue eyes, and tapped her chin with a thoughtful forefinger. "It's Jeff, isn't it?"

Linda looked at the older woman, at her sympathetic, well-intentioned expression, and knew she couldn't lie to her. "Yes."

Mrs. Gentry sighed, sitting on the leather divan across from Linda and folding her hands in her lap. "I thought so." She smiled dryly. "It's been awhile, but I can still recognize the signs. 'They do not love that do not show their love.' You were showing it quite distinctly last night, and if I'm not mistaken, so was Jeff. Hasn't he told you?"

"He's spending every free moment with Diana Northrup. That tells me all I need to know."

"Oh, you poor child. What are you going to do?"

"There is nothing I can do. It's out of my hands."

Mrs. Gentry's fingers gripped one another in agitation. "I do hope Jefferson isn't making a dreadful mistake. I love that boy so, I want him to be happy. He certainly deserves it, after the misery he suffered for so many years."

Linda's eyes darted to Mrs. Gentry's face, her attention caught. "What misery are you talking about? From what I can see, he's had the most pleasant of all possible lives, wealth, privilege, an indulgent family . . ."

Mrs. Gentry stared at her as if she had lost her mind. "An indulgent . . ." she began, and then patted the seat next to her on the couch. "Come here, my dear. I think there are some things about Jefferson you don't know."

Intrigued, Linda did as she was bid, and sat with her companion. The other woman poured a cup of tea from the chased silver service the servant had brought in while they were talking.

"Mrs. Jefferson Langford II is not Jeff's mother," she said. "He is the son of an Irish maid who was in the house in training. When it was discovered that the girl was pregnant by Jeff's father, she was sent away quietly until the baby was born. The Langfords took the child, and the girl went back to Derry. She died there when Jeff was about ten. As far as I know, he never saw her."

Linda sat, struck dumb, as Mrs. Gentry continued with the story. "Jeff's father wanted to keep the child— his only son, and a Langford, you see. By the time Jeff was born, his wife was too old to have any more children, and the other two were girls. So you might say he forced the whole family to accept the situation, and they weren't happy about it. Oh, the boy was sent to the best schools and had all the doors opened for him that one might expect, but he was always treated like a bit of a second-class citizen around the house. I saw some of that treatment personally, and it was the most exquisite form of cruelty. Cordelia Langford never let him forget that he wasn't quite up to the standards of her own children. He looked just like his mother, you understand, and every time Cory saw him, she saw her humiliation all over again. And Cory is proud, not a woman to take humiliation lightly."

Linda was silent, imagining the strawberry-blond-haired little boy like Cinderella with a wicked step-mother.

"His father was always good to him, but his father wasn't usually around. And the two girls—well, they were older, had their own lives, their own friends. But I heard the jokes about the son of a servant girl myself, and they weren't pretty."

"How many people know about his background?" Linda asked, finally finding her voice.

"Not that many, I would say, considering that it's over thirty years ago now, all water under the bridge. But I am certain it all made an indelible impression on Jefferson, one that formed his character and shaped his perceptions."

Things were falling into place now that had puzzled Linda before. Jeff's comment that first day, cautioning her not to make assumptions about his background that might be unwarranted, his willingness to give Linda a chance in the firm, his wistful remark at his house in Longmeadow about "happy families." How she must have hurt him, ranting on about the intolerance of the upper classes. No one knew it better than he.

"Does Diana Northrup know?"

"I'm sure she does. She is a sweet girl—it could hardly matter to her."

She was a sweet girl, and probably a large part of her attraction for Jeff lay in her spotless heritage. A step up, you might say, a not-so blueblood dating a thoroughbred. After the life he must have had, Linda could almost understand it.

"Why did you tell me this, Mrs. Gentry?"

"To help you, my dear. It won't be easy for you to see him with someone else, and I thought a little insight into the possible reasons for his choice might make the thing somewhat more tolerable. His father is quite old now, in his seventies, and has been retired for some time. I know he has been pressuring Jeff to settle down, to produce more grandchildren, get the succession going, you see. And I think it's reached the point where Jeff is giving in, and courting a suitable girl of whom his father would approve. He has always been anxious to earn that approval, as compensation of some sort, I imagine. A star athlete in school, top grades in college, all those things a father desires from his son, Jeff provided, probably hoping to wipe out the stigma of his birth."

And I certainly don't fit into that plan of stellar performance, Linda thought to herself. Mrs. Gentry was right. It did help to know this. It didn't make Jeff's behavior less painful, but it was less of a mystery now.

She glanced at her watch. "Mrs. Gentry, I have to go. I'm catching a flight at Logan at two, and I'll miss it if I don't call a cab right now."

"I won't hear of it. Ted will drive you out there. I'll send for him this minute."

Mrs. Gentry summoned the chauffeur, and Linda stood. "Thank you for the tea, and for the conversation. It was so good of you to tell me about Jeff. It helps more than you realize."

"I'm glad, Linda. If there is anything else I can do for you, please let me know."

Linda took her leave and was driven to the airport in limousined comfort. She arrived at Bradley in less than an hour, and was home by four.

There was a package waiting for her on her doorstep. As she let herself in, she ripped off the wrapper. The box bore the label of an expensive Boston shop, and inside was a cornflower-blue blouse of tissue-soft weave, hand stitched, that must have been expensive.

The card said, *"Je regrette."*

He was sorry. Sorry for what? That he had ruined her blouse, which didn't matter, or that he had ruined her life, which did?

———

Chapter Ten

THE PURITAN CASE came to court on Monday morning, and it went well. Jeff tried to talk to Linda at the break, and again at lunch, but she avoided him.

That afternoon, he cornered her in her office. "I'd like to speak with you," he said quietly.

Linda waited, capping her pen, amazed at her control.

"Why did you take off like that Saturday morning? I'm surprised you didn't leave a smoking trail in your wake. What happened?"

"I woke up to find myself in bed with the wrong person. It wasn't a place where I wanted to be."

"If that's the case, I was the wrong person all night long, too. It didn't seem to bother you then."

That was the sharpest thing he had ever said to Linda. It revealed that he was not as undisturbed by all that had happened as appearances might indicate. So it was possible to penetrate that bland exterior, and she had done it. That, at least, was something. He was upset. Linda knew him well enough now to tell that much.

"That's right," she answered evenly. "I was carried away on a tide of passion and regretted it in the morning. Surely you've had that experience."

"Not with you," he said, so softly that Linda couldn't be sure she had heard correctly. Did he mean . . . ? No, she must have been mistaken.

Jeff waited a moment, then leaned close to her, his green eyes exerting the same, unchanging spell as always. "So we close that chapter and move on to the next one, is that it?"

"That's right," Linda responded. "The chapter in which you go on your merry, philandering way and leave me alone."

Fury altered his handsome features, and Linda drew back, alarmed. She had never seen him like this.

He seized her by her shoulders and pulled her out of her chair. "I could shake you until your teeth rattle, but it wouldn't make you any less—"

"Independent?" she replied. "Principled?"

"Stubborn, opinionated, and *wrong*," he said, releasing her so suddenly that she rocked on her heels.

"What am I wrong about?" Linda asked, tilting her head back to look at him, her chin jutting forward pugnaciously. "I'm not wrong. Your problem is that you can't believe I'm not as dazzled by you as poor, hapless Diana. Well, counselor, I know you've never heard this before, but listen closely. Read my lips. *I don't want you.*"

Jeff grabbed her again, roughly, sinking his fingers into her hair, turning her face up to his.

"Don't you, Llhande? Don't you?"

She tried to pull away, but he held her fast, crushing her lips with his.

Once in his arms, she tried to fight, but desire soon

overtook her, as he had known it would. Hating her weakness, she kissed him back, eagerly. He ran his hands down her body, touching her everywhere, showing her that he could dominate her body even if he couldn't affect her feelings. She whimpered helplessly as he bent her over his arm and covered her throat and breast with burning kisses that seemed to scorch right through her clothes. Linda was dimly aware of the noises outside in the hall, beyond her door, and thought: what if someone comes in here and sees us? But nothing seemed to matter except the man who now made love to her, the closeness of him, his lips and his touch.

Suddenly, he let her go. She stumbled backwards, stunned.

"Now tell me you don't want me," he said triumphantly. But there was a catch in his voice that belied his exultation. Was she imagining it, or was he on the verge of breaking down? She dismissed the notion. It wasn't possible. Jefferson Langford would never lose his cool.

Linda tried a last, desperate lie. "That doesn't mean I love you," she said.

She saw the light go out of his face, to be replaced by defeat. "No, it doesn't," he agreed dully. "And that's the bottom line, isn't it?"

"That's the bottom line," she repeated, looking him straight in the eye, wanting to make sure he understood, so that he would not torment her further with these confrontations that went nowhere and didn't change the inevitable outcome.

He nodded slowly, dropped his gaze from hers, and left the room, shutting the door quietly behind him.

Jeff didn't bother her again. They spoke when they needed to discuss the case or when it concerned other matters involving the firm, but that was all. He seemed to have erased her effectively from his existence.

Linda was thoroughly miserable. She didn't know which was worse, having him offer the crumbs that kept her begging, or having him ignore her.

Christmas approached, and her lack of appetite for the holiday season made Linda feel like Scrooge. There is nothing worse than feeling extremely unhappy when everyone else is having a good time, and she felt isolated, alone. Since Christmas Eve fell on a Saturday, the office party was on Friday afternoon.

Linda had a drink with Craig and Susan, declining their offer to continue the celebration elsewhere, aware of Jeff and Diana on the other side of the room. The noise and hysterically cheerful music were giving her a headache. She listened to a group of secretaries discussing Jeff and his date. They were too charming for words, in the opinion of the onlookers.

Linda's headache became worse. She went out to the water cooler to get a drink so she could take some aspirin. On the way back to get her purse, Jeff stepped into her path.

She tried to brush past him, but he put his hand on her arm. "Linda, please."

She stopped.

"Linda, I want to apologize for the scene I made in your office the day we began the Puritan case. I realize I should have spoken to you about it before this, but to be honest, it's taken me some time to get up the courage to discuss it. My behavior was inexcusable, and I'm sorry."

Linda just wanted to get away from him. "It's all right, Jeff. We were both upset."

"I've never manhandled a woman that way in my life, and I've felt rotten about it ever since. I can't imagine what made me lose control like that. I hope you'll forgive me."

If he stood there looking at her like that much longer, she wouldn't be responsible for the consequences. "You're forgiven, Jeff. I wasn't exactly graciousness itself, either."

"We do seem to bring out the worst in each other on occasion," he said, watching her.

"Yes, we do. That's a good reason to limit the time we spend together," she answered lightly.

He took her hand and raised it to his lips. She looked down at the golden head bent over her fingers, and bit her lip. Why did he have to make this so very hard?

Jeff kissed her palm. "Have a happy holiday."

Oh, sure. Fat chance.

"The same to you, Jeff," Linda replied, and made her escape.

Numbly, Linda sat watching yet another rerun of *White Christmas*. She sipped a glass of wine as Bing Crosby and Rosemary Clooney fell in love, to the music of Irving Berlin. She was trying hard to believe that she would get over this, that the pain would someday fade and her life would return to normal. At the commercial break, the beaming news announcer chortled about the falling snow and an old-fashioned holiday, reminding her to tune in at eleven for details. "Don't hold your breath," Linda mumbled, and, turning on the porch light, went to the window.

A Currier and Ives scene met her eyes. The avenue was still silent under a blanket of white, with street lamps illuminating the cascading flakes and casting blue shadows on the deepening drifts. Linda could see a twinkling tree in the living room of the house across the way, framed by the sweep of heavy lace curtains. A large evergreen wreath, trailing a red velvet bow, showed in a spotlight set on the lawn. As she watched, the carved front door opened and a couple emerged, laughing, carrying festively wrapped packages. They slipped and slid in the driveway, loading their burdens into the rear of a station wagon. The man bent down and made a snowball, aiming it at his companion, who ducked and laughed delightedly, packing a projectile of her own. The fight continued until both were wet and covered with a fine, powdery frosting, like confectioners' sugar. Finally the man caught the woman and embraced her, kissing her while the snow filled in their footprints as they stood in the swirling storm. Still holding her close, the man ushered her into the passenger seat of the car, tucking a robe over her lap. Then he went around to the driver's side, and they drove off, on their way to the night's festivities. Linda let the curtain drop slowly and turned away.

She walked back to the fireplace and put on another log, then curled up on the sofa. It had been a mistake to refuse all invitations for this evening. She could have been at Maggie's party, or gone to Aunt Marie's early, or stayed with Laura and Charlie in Vermont. Instead she was watching old movies on Christmas Eve and feeling sorry for herself.

But she couldn't help it. She saw the beautiful couple again in her mind's eye, Diana in the green wool dress she had worn to the office party, Jeff in the dark jacket that set off his gold-red hair and light eyes to perfection. For the first time she gave in to the burden threatening to crush her and started to cry. It was such a release that she could not stop. Deep, wracking sobs shook her frame, and tears coursed down her cheeks and went into her mouth. She hadn't cried like this since childhood, when her parents died. There was no one to see her, and she let it all out, until, exhausted, she fell asleep.

* * *

The doorbell woke her. Confused, she thought the sound had come from the television, but she heard it again and realized what it was. *White Christmas* had been followed by *Going My Way*. Getting up to switch off the TV, Linda caught sight of herself in the mirror above the fireplace. Her eyes were red and swollen, her hair was in a tangle, and the blue velvet robe was crushed and rumpled. Oh, well. It was probably only Maggie, leaving her guests for a few minutes to check on her despondent friend.

Yawning and combing her hair with her fingers, Linda pulled open the door. Jefferson Langford stood on the porch, a brown leather overnight bag at his feet. "Merry Christmas," he said.

Linda stared at him as if he had just arrived from Venus. "You're in Boston," she said stupidly. She had assumed he would go to his father's house for the holiday.

"I don't think so," he replied, his eyes searching her face.

"What are you doing here?" she asked wretchedly, goaded beyond bearing by his sudden appearance. It was bad enough to think of him in the abstract, but seeing him in the flesh was unendurable.

"I have to talk to you," he said. "May I come in, or do I have to stand out here like Santa Claus making a bad entrance?"

Linda moved aside dazedly, unable to believe this was happening. Jeff tossed his bag onto the carpet and shut the door. Snowflakes were glistening in his hair and melting on his overcoat. His cheeks were flushed and his eyes sparkling from the cold. She was miserably conscious of the contrast between how good he looked and how bad she looked.

"You've been crying," he began. There was no point

in denying something that was patently obvious to all but the blind, so she went on the attack instead.

"Where's your girlfriend?" she questioned defensively.

"I assume you mean Diana. She's up in Boston with her mother," he said quietly.

"Why aren't you there too?"

"Because I want to be here with you."

"Because you want to . . . Jeff, what is going on?" she asked with a moan.

"I had a rather enlightening chat with Clara Gentry," he said softly. "She called me this afternoon."

Linda's eyes flew to his face. Oh, my God, he knew. Mrs. Gentry had told him.

"And," he continued, "I've come here to say that I love you and want you to marry me."

Linda sat down on the sofa, unable to speak.

He came and sat next to her, forcing her to look at him. He touched her cheek, his eyes filled with inexpressible tenderness.

"Linda, darling, why did you say nothing and let me go on thinking that you hated me?"

Linda felt the sting of more tears at the back of her throat, but they were tears of happiness this time.

"I thought you were using me," she said. "You could have anyone you wanted . . ."

He shook his head in gentle reprimand. "These past months, the only one I wanted was you."

"What about Diana? What does she want?"

"Diana wants a man who wants her. We talked all night after the office party. I saw your face as you were leaving, and so did she. I admitted that I loved you, but thought at that time that there was no hope for me. Then I heard from good old meddling Clara Gentry." He stroked Linda's hair. "Don't worry about Diana. She's a lovely woman with her pick of suitors. She'll find the right one. But it isn't me. She doesn't really love me." He paused, tracing the outline of her lips with a forefinger. "But you do, don't you?"

Linda's eyes closed. She nodded.

He pulled her into his arms, crushing her fiercely to him. "And I love you, my darling. Nothing is ever going to separate us again."

Linda suddenly remembered Mrs. Gentry's remarks about Jeff's seeking parental approval. "What will your father say, Jeff? I hardly have Diana's ... advantages."

He smiled. "Clara told you about him, eh?" The smile faded, replaced by a look of determination. "I'll handle him. My father has always done exactly as he pleased, and I shall do the same."

Linda stared at him, unable to credit this miracle.

He nuzzled her, kissing her neck, her hair, every place he could reach.

"Why?" he asked huskily. "Why didn't you tell me? One word from you would have done it. I waited, but that word never came. You really had me believing you detested me. You were so cold to me, either pretending I wasn't there or cutting me up with that rapier tongue."

"I guess I thought that if you really cared about me, you would come to me."

"Come to you! That would have taken more nerve than I'll ever possess. Look at it from my point of view. The first time we made love, at your house, the next day you treated me like someone you'd met at a convention."

"After I saw the announcement of your engagement," she reminded him.

"Diana's mother and I have discussed that," he said grimly. "There will be no further bulletins."

"I'm so glad."

"And," he went on, "the second time, at the hotel,

you vanished the next morning, leaving me a note that sounded like it was written by my nanny: 'Have a good time . . . see you at the office.'"

"After I found a note indicating that you were seeing a travel agent with Diana that day. I concluded that there was a romantic little trip in the offing."

He held her off to look at her, as if to see if she was serious, and then chuckled. "You goose. Diana was planning a surprise for her parents, an anniversary cruise on the *Queen Elizabeth II*. I went along only because I'm familiar with the ship, and she wanted to select the best accommodations."

"Oh," said Linda in a small voice.

He stroked her shoulders, as if by touching her constantly he could convince them both that they were not apart, as they had feared, but together.

"Well," he said, "to quote Rhett Butler in a similar situation, 'It seems we have been at cross purposes.' Thank God for Clara Gentry."

"She told me about your mother," Linda said. "I could have bitten my tongue off for some of the things I said."

He shushed her, kissing her quiet. "None of that matters now. I need you, Linda, more than I have the eloquence to say. And I mean to have you."

How she had wanted to hear those words. "Do you, Jeff? You've always seemed like a law unto yourself, needing no one."

"That's no longer true. Loneliness is a funny thing. You get used to it; it seems bearable, even normal, until you meet the one person who could make it disappear forever. And then if you can't have that one person, the loneliness multiplies, becomes intolerable. That's how I felt when I thought I couldn't have you—bereft."

She looked into the lovely green eyes and smiled. "You'll never get rid of me again."

His mouth moved to her throat, and his hands slipped inside her robe. "We'll get married as soon as we can get the blood tests and the papers," he whispered. "Let's talk about it later, okay?"

Her hands pulled at his clothes, and she murmured, "I want to go someplace warm and sunny for the honeymoon."

"Anything you say." He groaned, letting her wrap slip to the floor and burying himself in her softness.

Her last thought, before she lost herself in Jeff completely, was that she would finally get to see what he looked like with a tan.

Second Chance at Love™

____ 06195-6 **SHAMROCK SEASON #35** Jennifer Rose
____ 06304-5 **HOLD FAST TIL MORNING #36** Beth Brookes
____ 06282-0 **HEARTLAND #37** Lynn Fairfax
____ 06408-4 **FROM THIS DAY FORWARD #38** Jolene Adams
____ 05968-4 **THE WIDOW OF BATH #39** Anne Devon
____ 06400-9 **CACTUS ROSE #40** Zandra Colt
____ 06401-7 **PRIMITIVE SPLENDOR #41** Katherine Swinford
____ 06424-6 **GARDEN OF SILVERY DELIGHTS #42** Sharon Francis
____ 06521-8 **STRANGE POSSESSION #43** Johanna Phillips
____ 06326-6 **CRESCENDO #44** Melinda Harris
____ 05818-1 **INTRIGUING LADY #45** Daphne Woodward
____ 06547-1 **RUNAWAY LOVE #46** Jasmine Craig
____ 06423-8 **BITTERSWEET REVENGE #47** Kelly Adams
____ 06541-2 **STARBURST #48** Tess Ewing
____ 06540-4 **FROM THE TORRID PAST #49** Ann Cristy
____ 06544-7 **RECKLESS LONGING #50** Daisy Logan
____ 05851-3 **LOVE'S MASQUERADE #51** Lillian Marsh
____ 06148-4 **THE STEELE HEART #52** Jocelyn Day
____ 06422-X **UNTAMED DESIRE #53** Beth Brookes
____ 06651-6 **VENUS RISING #54** Michelle Roland
____ 06595-1 **SWEET VICTORY #55** Jena Hunt
____ 06575-7 **TOO NEAR THE SUN #56** Aimee Duvall
____ 05625-1 **MOURNING BRIDE #57** Lucia Curzon
____ 06411-4 **THE GOLDEN TOUCH #58** Robin James
____ 06596-X **EMBRACED BY DESTINY #59** Simone Hadary
____ 06660-5 **TORN ASUNDER #60** Ann Cristy
____ 06573-0 **MIRAGE #61** Margie Michaels
____ 06650-8 **ON WINGS OF MAGIC #62** Susanna Collins

All of the above titles are $1.75 per copy

Available at your local bookstore or return this form to:

SECOND CHANCE AT LOVE
Book Mailing Service, P.O. Box 690, Rockville Cntr., NY 11570

Please send me the titles checked above. I enclose _____.
Include 75¢ for postage and handling if one book is ordered; 50¢ per book for
two to five. If six or more are ordered, postage is free. California, Illinois, New
York and Tennessee residents please add sales tax.

NAME _____

ADDRESS _____

CITY_____ STATE/ZIP_____

Allow six weeks for delivery.   SK-41

_____ 05816-5 **DOUBLE DECEPTION #63** Amanda Troy

_____ 06675-3 **APOLLO'S DREAM #64** Claire Evans

_____ 06680-X **THE ROGUE'S LADY #69** Anne Devon

_____ 06687-7 **FORSAKING ALL OTHERS #76** LaVyrle Spencer

_____ 06689-3 **SWEETER THAN WINE #78** Jena Hunt

_____ 06690-7 **SAVAGE EDEN #79** Diane Crawford

_____ 06691-5 **STORMY REUNION #80** Jasmine Craig

_____ 06692-3 **THE WAYWARD WIDOW #81** Anne Mayfield

_____ 06693-1 **TARNISHED RAINBOW #82** Jocelyn Day

_____ 06694-X **STARLIT SEDUCTION #83** Anne Reed

_____ 06695-8 **LOVER IN BLUE #84** Aimée Duvall

_____ 06696-6 **THE FAMILIAR TOUCH #85** Lynn Lawrence

_____ 06697-4 **TWILIGHT EMBRACE #86** Jennifer Rose

_____ 06698-2 **QUEEN OF HEARTS #87** Lucia Curzon

_____ 06850-0 **PASSION'S SONG #88** Johanna Phillips

_____ 06851-9 **A MAN'S PERSUASION #89** Katherine Granger

_____ 06852-7 **FORBIDDEN RAPTURE #90** Kate Nevins

_____ 06853-5 **THIS WILD HEART #91** Margarett McKean

_____ 06854-3 **SPLENDID SAVAGE #92** Zandra Colt

_____ 06855-1 **THE EARL'S FANCY #93** Charlotte Hines

_____ 06858-6 **BREATHLESS DAWN #94** Susanna Collins

_____ 06859-4 **SWEET SURRENDER #95** Diana Mars

_____ 06860-8 **GUARDED MOMENTS #96** Lynn Fairfax

_____ 06861-6 **ECSTASY RECLAIMED #97** Brandy LaRue

_____ 06862-4 **THE WIND'S EMBRACE #98** Melinda Harris

_____ 06863-2 **THE FORGOTTEN BRIDE #99** Lillian Marsh

_____ 06864-0 **A PROMISE TO CHERISH #100** LaVyrle Spencer

_____ 06865-9 **GENTLE AWAKENING #101** Marianne Cole

_____ 06866-7 **BELOVED STRANGER #102** Michelle Roland

_____ 06867-5 **ENTHRALLED #103** Ann Cristy

_____ 06868-3 **TRIAL BY FIRE #104** Faye Morgan

_____ 06869-1 **DEFIANT MISTRESS #105** Anne Devon

All of the above titles are $1.75 per copy

Available at your local bookstore or return this form to:

SECOND CHANCE AT LOVE
Book Mailing Service, P.O. Box 690, Rockville Cntr., NY 11570

Please send me the titles checked above. I enclose _____.
Include 75¢ for postage and handling if one book is ordered: 50¢ per book for
two to five. If six or more are ordered, postage is free. California, Illinois, New
York and Tennessee residents please add sales tax.

NAME _____

ADDRESS _____

CITY_____ STATE ZIP_____

Allow six weeks for delivery.   SK-41

WHAT READERS SAY ABOUT
SECOND CHANCE AT LOVE BOOKS

"Your books are the greatest!"
—*M. N., Carteret, New Jersey**

"I have been reading romance novels for quite some time, but the SECOND CHANCE AT LOVE books are the most enjoyable."
—*P. R., Vicksburg, Mississippi**

"I enjoy SECOND CHANCE [AT LOVE] more than any books that I have read and I do read a lot."
—*J. R., Gretna, Louisiana**

"For years I've had my subscription in to Harlequin. Currently there is a series called Circle of Love, but you have them all beat."
—*C. B., Chicago, Illinois**

"I really think your books are exceptional ... I read Harlequin and Silhouette and although I still like them, I'll buy your books over theirs. SECOND CHANCE [AT LOVE] is more interesting and holds your attention and imagination with a better story line ..."
—*J. W., Flagstaff, Arizona**

"I've read many romances, but yours take the 'cake'!"
—*D. H., Bloomsburg, Pennsylvania**

"Have waited ten years for *good* romance books. Now I have them."
—*M. P., Jacksonville, Florida**

*Names and addresses available upon request